The Short Story Factory

Hugo Hanriot

The Short Story Factory

ISBN 978-1470086541

CONTACT: hhanriot@yahoo.com

Cover & Interior Design by Ellen C. Maze, The Author's Mentor , http://www.ellencmaze.com

PRINTED IN THE UNITED STATES OF AMERICA

Heartfelt thanks to my wife Sabina for allowing me to take time away from her to write these stories.

Also deep thanks and sincere gratitude to my dear friends and proofreaders: Marie McDonell, Laura Swidersky, Rebecca Knight, Hugo Hanriot Jr. and Tim Dando.

DEAR Raymond & LAURA,

THANKS FOR YOUR FRIENDSHIP AND FOR LAURA SKILLFUL PROOFREADING. WITHOUT YOUR SUPPORT this BOOK wouldn't be.

Hugo Hanriot

April, 2012

Table of Contents

1

Me, Her, Drunk?

HE WAS JUST AN ILL-EDUCATED YOUNG man without ambition or talent. Donald's only asset was his sister Sophie, a stunning, pretty girl too busy with burdening responsibility to acknowledge her own beauty. Their mother, tired for years of her husband's alcohol addiction, left them. Sophie filled the void at home by their mother's departure. She not only had resigned to accept her father's irresponsible boozing behavior but totally took on the parental responsibility for her next-to-useless 20-year-old brother.

Sophie had to shelve her desire to pursue a higher education. Pressed by their precarious economic situation, she looked for a job and found it at the zoo; her attractiveness and pleasant personality got her hired to work the information booth to assist visitors, lost children, and tourists. The pay wasn't great but, combined with the 'state assistance for low income families', it made life more livable. As she settled in her workplace, she thought about getting a job for her brother at the zoo. It wouldn't be easy; Donald had barely graduated from high school after repeating his last year twice. He had shown no interest in getting work after graduation.

Sophie attracted the attention of Greg, a volunteer that worked as a media relation officer for the zoo – he was the son of one of the most generous contributors to the zoo. The polished, wealthy young man, as he eyed Sophie, was hypnotized by her beauty and her unassuming personality. His love for the humble girl from the information booth grew fast; regardless of her family background, he proposed to her and she accepted.

The zoo director looked at the young man he had in front of his desk with mistrust; the body language of the young job seeker displayed complete disinterest, and his speech was so deficient that it caused irritation. Donald, instead of applying for a job in the zoo's Human Resources, had been brought straight to the director by Donald's new brother-in-law. Under normal circumstances, the zoo director wouldn't accept interviews for job applicants; he had instituted rigorous standards for Human Resources to follow when selecting new personnel. But this was a unique situation; Donald's sister was now the wife of Greg. Dissimulating his displeasure, he reluctantly authorized Human Resources to hire Donald as assistant keeper in the birds section – the zoo could afford the escape of a bird rather than a lion, he reasoned, annoyed by his decision.

The caretakers of the birds pavilion, when they met Donald, felt as if their respectable profession had reverted back to the days when the only requirement to be an animal-keeper was to be able to just clean up after the animals and to feed them. The zoo director seemed to ignore their backgrounds and rigorous training as records keepers, keen observers of animal behavior and public educators to the millions of visitors to the birds' pavilion. They resented working with Donald so much that, besides assigning him to clean the bird cages, they ordered him to feed the troublesome pair of bald eagles, notorious for their aggressiveness. They thought it would be a genius move to get even with him.

"The bald eagles are chasing Donald out of their cage," the bird supervisor reported to the zoo director days later. "They resent that Donald has forgotten many times to feed them. We also noticed he has a serious drinking problem; he should be fired."

"If I do, we'll lose Greg's family donations for the zoo's captive breeding endangered species program," the director explained to him.

"I have an idea," replied the supervisor. "Donald confessed to one of us about panicking when around snakes. If you could transfer him to the reptiles building he may want to quit."

Donald was told that for his own sake he was going to be transferred to another section of the zoo. To his dismay he wound up in the World of Reptile building. He had promised Sophie and Greg that he was going to try his best to keep his zoo job. The only way to calm down his fear of the snakes – and keep his promise – was tapping more into the cheap wine he hid every day in his lunch box concealed in a Coca-Cola bottle. He reasoned that if nobody had noticed his drinking problem in the bird section, they shouldn't notice it here either.

The half-lit room with the cobra's exhibit, at feeding time was closed to the public; the zoo fed them with frozen rats which had caused vomiting among some visitors who had witnessed that. It became the perfect time for Donald to taste his wine. He had noticed that any time he sipped wine from his Coca-Cola bottle, a young Egyptian cobra name Kissy approached him from inside her glass cage. Wanting to tease Kissy, Donald tied a string to the plastic cup filled with wine and lowered it into the cage. Kissy, at the beginning, would cautiously curl her body around the cup, lifting her head and flicking her tongue to smell the wine. After a few days she was sinking her head into the cup consuming almost as much wine as Donald – they had become drinking pals!

The news spread fast through the media; a venomous cobra had escaped from her cage and disappeared! The reptile exhibit was immediately closed to the public for safety reasons.

Five days after she escaped, keepers from the Reptile building discovered Donald lying in the dimly dark corner bench with Kissy on top of him smelling his mouth. Both were found highly intoxicated.

Later, when Donald saw pictures of the

incident, he fell into a deep shock that sent him to the hospital for days. After leaving the hospital, he noticed that his craving for alcohol had vanished. Meantime, The Wildlife Conservation Club had been awaiting his release from the hospital to award him with a medal of honor for his valiant action to entice the cobra to consume alcohol thus facilitating her capture and future well-being.

2

The Pickup Artist

"WHAT IS A PICKUP ARTIST?" SYLVIA'S mother asked. She was leery about her Texas born daughter dating a foreigner; a young man with an angelical smile and diabolical piercing eyes. Sylvia was the only success that her bum ex-husband ever accomplished during their marriage. Her daughter's silhouette, long legs, smooth curves, and radiant face should have been the masterpiece of a famous sculptor and not the product of a louse like him.

Sylvia's natural beauty had opened her many doors for a happy and successful life. In spite of marriage proposals from established wealthy young Texans, collecting three beauty contest crowns, and an offer to pose for a renowned modeling agency, she had instead opted for a quiet secretarial job in an insurance company.

Next month Sylvia was going to hit her thirtieth birthday. Then, from out of nowhere, appeared the young English rogue, who not only captured Sylvia's heart, but charmed the state of Texas by advertising himself as, "Andrew – The Great Seducer" and offering with it his video "Andrew, Make Out in Just One Minute."

"It seems to me like your new boyfriend runs a kinky business," her mother commented.

"Andrew provides a social service. He helps people to meet, date, and form friendships. I don't see anything wrong with that."

"I just can't understand why after refusing marriage from so many decent men you settle for a dubious stranger with a weird job."

"When Andrew said to me, 'If I could marry you, I envision growing old together and still finding you the hottest and most perfect woman of all,' I knew then he was the right man for me."

"Your father used to talk to me like that – and to every other woman he crossed paths with. Please, be careful with your new boyfriend."

Already having a master's degree in psychology Andrew decided to take "pickup lessons". He found the London lessons full of corny pick-up lines, insincere and fake. He decided to create his own methods. Since then, he had become a very successful "pickup professor".

Andrew conducted full house workshops in the major Texas cities. Sylvia quit her secretarial job to be with him. She assisted him as she attended his first workshop, "Secrets of Dating Younger Women", which lasted three evenings. Andrew, in a tasteful way, involved her in the demonstrations. The all-male class enjoyed her presence, opening up and confessing to her their inhibitions and weaknesses toward pretty younger women. Sylvia's participation was such a success that Andrew, impressed by the smartness of his Texan love, proposed to her. She asked him for time to think it over.

Next day they continued with the second workshop, "Secrets of Dating Older Women" which lasted just one evening. The third one, "Techniques for Older Women to Date Younger Men", had such a large female attendance "of cougars" that the class had to be held in a larger auditorium, and lasted a week. Here Andrew shone as a big star.

From Texas, the workshops moved to L.A., California, where Andrew planned to have the classes filmed as future video lessons.

In "Secrets of Dating Younger Women" Sylvia, now competent in her roll, stepped down from the stage to ask the all- male audience to share their inhibitions with her. After listening patiently and sympathizing with them, she gave her audience smart common sense tips. On stage, Andrew smiled his approval.

As she approached the next man, he lifted his head and looked straight at Sylvia. "I'm going to describe to you my problem referring back to the most beautiful moments of my life. There was this pretty young girl that I fell in love with from the moment I saw her. I was in an unhappy marriage at that time. Out of respect for the younger girl, and also fearful of her rejection, I decided to love her from a distance. I had no children, could easily file for divorce to pursue her, but she was surrounded by eligible young men that made me feel I had no chance to win her heart. Later I met her at a mutual friend's party. We talked, laughed and even danced. I was in heaven when I noticed there definitely was chemistry between us. Since my suppression of feelings toward her was becoming too painful, I requested a job transfer to Los Angeles. Now that I'm divorced and available, if I meet her again, what would you advise me to do?"

Sylvia, visibly shaken and tearful, embraced and kissed him. "In my dreams I saw you coming back to me," she said. "I declined many marriage opportunities hoping for this moment."

Andrew, speechless for the first time in his life, saw the only woman he had fallen madly in love with, leave the auditorium holding hands with the stranger.

3

The Genius' Jump

REUBEN TURNED AROUND LOOKING FOR the cup of coffee he had just made. He couldn't find it in the kitchen. Did I leave it in the bathroom? It wasn't in the bathroom either. Damn it! Let me check the bedroom. Before leaving the bathroom, he took a glanced at himself in the medicine cabinet's mirror. It surprised him to see how his forehead had been receding. With the rest of his hair in disarray, thick lenses; incisive, curiously bright eyes, and his tall, thin figure, he could pass for a geek, a bum or a crazy man. Either way, he had aged too fast for his being 26 years of age.

The lobby buzzer shook him out of his contemplation. "Sir, your driver just came in." He went down to the lobby.

His driver accompanied Reuben to the car. After closing the car door behind Reuben, the driver returned to the building and – as instructed by his bosses – went to check Reuben's apartment.

In the kitchen he found one of the stove burners turned on, the sink faucet running, and also discovered inside the refrigerator the cup of coffee Reuben couldn't find. He turned out the lights left on the kitchen, bathroom and bedroom, took Reuben's coat and gloves and left.

As they drove toward the first traffic light, Reuben said, "You reached this corner in 2 minutes. Considering the snow, traffic and type of gas you're using, it's very consistent with your style of driving." There was no response from the driver, just a smile. Reuben was a good guy, but just too weird for him!

The car stopped in front of the Hedge Fund Firm's building. Reuben felt his heart pumping harder. They had assigned Ethel to assist him with his office and personal needs. He had strong feelings for her. She would welcome him with his breakfast ready, and once a week takes care of his dirty laundry (collected by the driver at his apartment). Also she would shave him, trim his hair when needed, join him for his office lunch, attend the phone, and patiently listen the rumblings of his mind boggled with mathematical calculation deciding the firm's investment moves. His crunching trading data results had made the Hedge Fund the most successful firm in Wall Street in the commodities and currency trades.

Besides the personal care of the "Genius", Ethel served as his liaison with the rest of the company. Since no one was allowed inside Reuben's office (it was Reuben's strict orders) she conveyed to him all the messages from the directors and employees. Also she received the data from the firm's technical departments: weather reports, government's stability, monetary crisis, inflation, psychological political crisis and market indicators around the world. Reuben would feed his mind, and his computers with the data. "I'm like a fortune teller," Reuben would comment to Ethel. "I mix all this data into my formulas and predict the future."

"You are a genius," she would respond with genuine admiration.

To Reuben, Ethel's voice always sounded like sweet music. After working together for almost a year, she had opened up, confiding to him her two failed marriages and her break up with her last boyfriend. Ethel was ten years older than him, but he didn't care. He had fallen madly in love with her. It was the first time in his life that he had felt such a strong emotion for a woman; just sensing her around made him feel more human. He wanted – but was too scared – to ask her to move in with him. So far they had attended several rock concerts together, dined at diverse ethnic restaurants and went to see foreign films. He had even ventured to kiss Ethel on her cheek during some of the movies.

Later that morning, Reuben's world shattered when Ethel received a call, she grabbed her coat and abruptly left the office. "I have to see him," she had said running out the door.

Disturbed by jealousy, thinking Ethel was going to see her former boyfriend, Reuben went home. Some time ago, one of the elevator repair men had told him the speed of the elevator; using it, he had calculated his floor height. "It's high enough," he said before leaping out the front window of his apartment.

Reuben awoke in the hospital. He was full of pain; otherwise, he was okay. He had landed on a mountain of trash bags that had piled up since the last weeks blizzard (the sanitation workers had been in a slowdown because of overtime cuts). Ethel was seating next to his bed, holding his bandaged hand.

"I cannot leave you alone any longer," she whispered in his ear. "I went to assist my brother who fell ill, and look what you did. From now on, I'm going to move-in and care for you 24 hours a day."

Reuben's swollen lips drew an instant smile.

4

Sean's War

AS SEAN GREW, SO DID RON AND MARGARET'S concern for him. Their son had a severe speech impediment and was also uncoordinated; otherwise, he was a bright, handsome kid.

"Our son is fine, his speech problem is treatable," Ron tried to calm Margaret's worries. "Our mistake is we keep trying to compare him to his sister."

"It hurts hearing him stutter and seeing he stumbled around, while Joan wins medals in gymnastics and excels in her school's plays."

"He needs to gain confidence. I'm going to take him back for baseball practice. When we played a while ago he showed a strong arm and seemed to enjoy it."

"It's apparent the school special education programs haven't improved his speech at all. I'm going to have Sean tutored privately for speech therapy," added Margaret not too convinced that baseball was the solution.

Ron needed a lot of persuasion to get Sean out there pitching again. He thought his son, being a left-hander, would have some advantage over the other kids. But although he threw good fast balls, his clumsiness affected his accuracy. Sean was less than enthusiastic when his father signed him up to play in the 8-to-10 year old Little League team. His erratic pitching brought on funny looks from his teammates. He quit after a few games.

Sean showed no improvement at all with the additional speech therapy. "Your son's stuttering may be rooted in some kind of early psychological problem," the therapist conveyed to Margaret. "Did he have any major trauma during his early infancy?"

"Not that we are aware of," Margaret said after a long pause.

Ron and she were working couples; Sean had been cared by Margaret's sister, Blanche, during his early years. Her sister was a wonderful woman. Despite her physical limitation with her legs, she took good care of Sean. But, why was Sean so different from Joan? Margaret had enjoyed being a full time mother with her daughter; she had breastfed and cared for Joan exclusively in her first years of existence. She sang, played, and dressed her as a doll until she entered pre-school. Then she got pregnant with Sean. Having two children to care for, there was need for additional income, and she went back to work. That was when Ron and her agreed to have Blanche baby sit Sean.

Sean started sixth grade with bigger problems in school. A group of kids begun making fun of his stuttering and pushed him around.

"I know you believe doctors can treat our son," Ron said to his wife, "but now it's a different matter. Our son is being beaten up at school, and is coming home with fat lips. I'm going to take him to an academy that teaches self-defense."

Bill was a high school friend of Ron. He had enlisted in the army, where he became an instructor of martial arts. When he retired from the Armed Forces, he opened a gym to train and develop professional kick boxers. He also worked with children to teach them self-defense and self-esteem.

Bill warmly welcomed his pal Ron with an embrace and a big smile. Then he turned to Sean, "Hi kiddo, nice to meet you."

After remembering their shared anecdotes from high school, Ron addressed the main purpose of his visit, "Sean is being bullied by a group of kids at the school. We need your help."

"Hey Sean, I got news for you. Your father and I were also bullied at school. We got together to fight them. The bullies are insecure and scared of facing somebody tougher than them. They always pick on kids that look like easy prey. I can build your self-esteem to the point that they will be scared of bothering you. How would you like that?"

"I like it." Sean's prompt response surprised Ron. His son had shouted it without stumbling in his words.

Sean's improvement became clear to Ron and

Margaret. Bill opened his martial arts classes with meditation. According to him, it developed the brain to work at the same pace as the mouth and other body parts. Then he did yoga as a warm up, followed by strength exercises to develop powerful blows and leg kicks. It worked miracles with their son. Sean's speech was more consistent and his body's coordination and timing were improving.

That evening the junior high school presented the last play of the year. The auditorium was packed with parents and students. Joan had an important role in the play. Sean, at the insistence of the drama teacher and the encouragement of his family, had a limited role with no dialogue. Being the only male player, they assigned him a class room near the auditorium to change into his costume. He was sweating after his first entrance on stage. He walked to change his outfit. As he got to the classroom the three bullies that had tortured him for so long jumped him. They immediately noticed Sean wasn't scared. He needed a good beating to become submissive again. One bully head locked him from the back; the other two were punching him from the front.

Sean heard Aunt Blanche's hysteric scream, "Stop bad baby! Don't even dare get out of your chair! You are killing my legs!" Aunt Blanche's voice suddenly turned weak, then silenced. He had knocked down the two bullies in front with legs kicks; the one holding him from behind flew over his head and landed on his back.

"You S.O.B. give me your iPods. I know you

called me a faggot on the internet." They obeyed.

Sean smashed the three I-Pods, changed into his costume, and left the bullies lying on the floor, crying in pain.

5

Hipolito's Showmanship

RAY AND SUSIE WERE A HAPPY COUPLE. Hipolito, their adopted son, was the light of their lives. In their eyes Hipolito could do no wrong – they just loved him the same as if he was the son that Susie couldn't conceive. They respected his different moods: sometimes warm, looking for their attention; sometimes indifferent, ignoring them.

When his owners entertained their friends; Hipolito, driven by his show-off personality, would make his nonchalant entrance in the living room faking surprise, like saying, "I didn't know you guys were here."

He would stand still with his long tail pointing to the ceiling inviting the visitors to admire his athletic body wrapped in his all thick white long hair — he knew he looked adorable!

He would then step forward with an aloof walk, take a short run, and jump over to Susie's lap.

Susie with a sweet smile would pet her cat child's head. He would curl his tail like a question mark and look at Susie through his dreamy half-shut green eyes enchanted by her touch. It was a picture of genuine-mutual-tender love that would last until Hipolito would notice in Ray's face his need for attention too. He would then, with an athletic jump, land on Ray's shoulder. Loud cheers from the guests would celebrate his acrobatics.

"Why did you name such a sweetie 'Hipolito'?" a woman at the party asked Susie.

"It was his name when we adopted him from the shelter. Ray and I consulted a psychologist friend who thought changing his name was going to confuse him."

When their guests would start chatting, drinking and eating, the attention toward Hipolito faded away. Hipolito, spoiled beyond belief, would descend from Ray's shoulder to the floor and untie the men's shoelaces, provoking loud laughs.

One day Hipolito learned the hard way that life wasn't always fun. He had awakened with a sharp pain in his back and could barely move. His worried owners rushed him to the animal clinic, where he was diagnosed partially paralyzed by a spinal-cord injury. Susie broke out in tears as she cradled him in her arms. Luckily, Hipolito's condition didn't require surgery.

"There is a rehabilitation center nearby where he can be treated," the neurologist at the clinic tried to calm Susie. "The therapy is used in humans and dogs, but it's worth trying it with your cat. It involves physical therapy in water."

"How expensive is that treatment," Ray asked him. "With this economy my job is no longer secure."

"We are both professionals with good jobs. If one of us becomes unemployed we will still manage okay," interceded Susie.

As Susie decided, Hipolito began his therapy. Ray – just laid off from work – took him every morning to the animal rehabilitation center. As expected, at the beginning it was hard to get Hipolito inside the water tank. He became an "ordinary" cat, he hated getting wet! Ray, patiently, started to rub his body with warm wet hands, and then slightly submerged his resisting paws in the tank. Little by little Hipolito adjusted and began to enjoy feeling the warm water. He tried to dog-paddle to keep afloat. It didn't take long for him to swim across the tank over and over again, fully enjoying the cheers of Ray, the therapist and the clinic receptionist – his showman personality had revived again!

It was the last visit to the animal clinic for what had been Hipolito's amazing recovery. On their way back home, when stopped at a red light, Ray in total disbelief saw his cat jump out of the car through a less than half open window and run full gallop toward the park pool. Ray parked the car and chased him. When he reached the pool he saw Hipolito on the diving board ready to jump, encouraged by an enthusiastic crowd.

Hipolito faked several short runs as if to jump, pulling back at the last instant to the crowd's delight.

He was also a clown! Finally, timing the jump perfectly, Hipolito made three somersaults before softly entering ears first into the water. The crowd went wild. He rose to the surface and with a quick dog-paddle swim reached the pool's ladder, got out and climbed the diving board tower again.

Minutes later a video of Hipolito diving into the park pool had invaded the internet sites. By then Ray received a fine for taking an animal into the public pool; his name, address and telephone number was written on the ticket. A lifeguard had caught Hipolito and handed him to Ray's open arms. Holding the cat's wet body tightly against his chest, he walked back to his car. When he got home the phone was ringing off the hook. Sportswear manufacturers, TV talk shows, show business and movie agents wanted to hire the diving cat.

6

Amazon's Illegal Matter

THEY WERE FIRST SPOTTED BY A MILITARY plane in a remote part of the Peruvian Amazon. The Government of Peru announced: "The Peruvian Army air surveillance tracked a tiny group of men, women and children that lived unexposed to regular civilization. Aerial photos of the small tribe showed naked men, women and children fishing and bathing in the river, unaffected by the brutal Amazonian sun and stinging insects."

"Survival International" was authorized to join the Peruvian Army in their effort to learn more about the indigenous tribesman.

They were again spotted in Las Piedras, Peru, in the south-eastern Amazon. Terrified, they ran to their shelters on the beach to hide from the plane. During the second pass, one of the women carrying a small boy pointed aggressively toward the plane with an arrow, while the rest of the group sought refuge in the forest.

The Peruvian Authorities were aware of the existence of illegal mahogany loggers which posed a threat to the tribe. They airlifted a command to the jungle, two doctors of the Peruvian army, and a husband and wife anthropology team from “Survival International”. They landed by helicopter on the spot where the tribe had been seen. To their dismay, they found a large patch of the jungle that extended along the river, depleted of its trees, and hundreds of illegally cut mahogany logs hidden close by for future travel downstream. The loggers had left in a rush, leaving their tools behind. In one of their makeshift huts the army found three young native girls tied to a post. They were naked, shivering and had symptoms of high fever. One of them was vomiting.

“Criminals!” the commanding officer exploded with rage. “These children are no older than ten.” He ordered his men to search for the loggers. “These animals have raped these girls! I order my troops to shoot to kill if they spot them! I suspect the natives we found shot to death around this hut came to rescue these girls. Their arrows were no match for these butchers’ guns!”

After checking the girls, the doctors determined they were all raped and suffering from malaria. The vicious sexual contact of the loggers had contaminated the girls with their “civilized virus”. The three girls were flown to the Military Hospital in Lima in a desperate attempt to save them. Only one survived. She was immediately vaccinated to protect her from the new world contaminations.

The anthropologist couple was authorized by the Peruvian Government to take the girl to a university in California. They were interested in researching her adaptation to the civilized world, and learn the origin of her native language. Once they were settled in an apartment inside the university's complex, the couple worked hard in gaining the girl's trust. She would spend all day hidden in the apartment crying, probably remembering the loggers' abuse.

Everyday, language experts would show the girl simple objects, simultaneously pronouncing its English names, hoping she would identify them in her native language. In less than a year, Hope – as they named her – was speaking and writing English as an American child of her age. She was smart; her mind was ready to absorb new knowledge. In exchange, the language experts only got from her a few guttural sounds of no meaning.

The university, surprised by the fast assimilation of Hope to her civilized environment, gave her crash courses in subjects that children of her age were taught in their school curriculums. When the instructors felt she was ready, they sent her to school. Hope joined her classmates, anxious to make friends. The traumatized girl from the Amazon seemed as normal as them; only in the privacy of her apartment did she suffer horrible childhood flashbacks. During those moments, the anthropologist couple was always able to calm her down; she had become like their daughter.

After graduating from the university as a

registered nurse, Hope moved in with her boyfriend, Raul, a young man of Hispanic parents who had just graduated from law school. Because of his status as the son of illegal parents, he could not take the California State Bar examination.

"I would like to marry you." Raul proposed to Hope. "I found work as a paralegal in an attorney's office. As soon as I get my citizenship, I would work as an attorney and provide you with a comfortable life."

She accepted gladly; although, when gathering their documentation, a major surprise shook their plans – Hope's special guest invitation to reside in United States had expired.

"At this moment we're both illegal residents, exposed to be deported," Raul explained to her. "Our future is very uncertain. The Dream Act bill in support of people like us to gain citizenship has just been vetoed in Congress. If we have children, they could be deported as well."

"We don't have another place to go; this is home," Hope stated firmly. "We'll get marry and hope for things to change."

7

Three Strikes

TIM DID TIME IN THE SLAMMER TWICE. He was just free and trying hard to find work. Without a trade or family support, and two black marks on his record, he knew it would take a miracle for him to get a decent job. He also knew it was too risky to go back to selling drugs. Tim had been warned that with a third strike, New Jersey (as well as other states) was enforcing longer periods of incarceration for repeat felony offenders. The days of driving an expensive flashy car, living in a luxurious apartment, blowing money at casinos in Atlantic City, and getting broads at the wink of his eye, were gone.

After a couple months of trying to get a job, Tim landed one with the help of an organization that assisted ex-inmates. He was hired by a moving company to load and unload trucks. Every day he put in long hours sweating, lifting and moving heavy pieces of furniture. At night he would return to his rented room, jump in bed, and sleep until the next day, and then do it all over again. Was that the "freedom" he dreamed of in prison? Now he understood why Joel smiled at him in disbelief when he explained his plan to rebuild his life as a free, honest man.

Tim and Joel had become good friends after a prison sergeant moved Tim into Joel's cell. They respected each other's space and privacy; when they wanted, they would engage in intelligent, thoughtful conversation.

Joel, in his mid-fifties, was serving the tenth year of a life sentence for killing his mistress. During those ten years he immersed himself in legal books about criminal, civil, and court procedures. He had become the "prison lawyer", the one the inmates would approach for writing parole applications, requests for new court hearings to reduce their sentences, or for challenging the prosecutors' evidence used against them. Besides helping the fellow inmates, he also advised the prison staff with their legal problems.

Tim had shared the many privileges Joel received from the prison staff. In their cell they had an electric grill to cook their own meals, a large TV and a computer, plus the trust and respect of both the inmates and guards. They enjoyed cooking special dinners with the food gifts from the families of inmates and the prison personnel that Joel had helped.

Tim paid Joel a visit as soon as he saved

enough money for the train and the taxi fare to get to the prison. The two former cellmates embraced, happy to meet again.

"How is life treating you?" Joel asked, smiling, glad to see his old roommate.

"Life can be tougher outside than in here; sometimes I wish I have never left the slammer." Tim talked about the low pay and hard, back-breaking job he had. "I've thought about going back to drug selling."

"You're too smart for that. Listen, I've been helping a new inmate with his legal papers. He's a big time drug dealer. He told me his people found a way to sell imitation herbal grass that produces the same effects as real marijuana. It's a great business with no legal repercussions."

"That's ideal for a guy in my situation."

"I'll tell this guy I'm going to help him with the papers to reduce his sentence in half if he sets you up with his outside connections to sell the legal weed."

"And how could I repay you for it?

"Remember the broad I killed? She left two kids; one of them is my son. I want you to split up the money you make; half for you, and the other half for my two kids."

As agree, Tim was set up with a large piece of territory as the King Pin distributor of the legal hybrid bud. The herb was sold by his crew to teenagers that drove from the suburbs to buy what they thought was authentic marijuana. Money started to flow in as if were good old days. Tim drove to visit Joel in his new sport car every week, to account for the money he had sent to Joel's sister; she was raising his two teens.

That morning, Tim and his new girlfriend descended from his apartment to the building's garage, planning to spend a few days trying their luck at the Atlantic City casinos. He carried their luggage; she followed him. Suddenly, she heard shots and jumped for cover. After she heard the shooters' car take off, she came out of hiding and saw Tim lying dead in a pool of blood.

Later she learned that a member of a new gang trying to take control of Tim's territory had confessed to killing him. Meanwhile, at the prison, Joel and his friends waited for the arrival of Tim's killer to take care of him.

Bite! Bite! Bite!

CUCA, A LONG-LEGGED PERUVIAN teenaged beauty, had captured the USA modeling world with her smooth bronze skin, soft curves, black vivacious eyes, shiny coal black hair, radiant smile, and natural poise. Besides her physical attributes she was also bright. Her mother – a typical and traditional loving mother – made it her main mission to shield her attractive teenager from the many admirers. It was quite a difficult task for a parent coming from a different culture still unfamiliar with American upbringing and customs.

Cuca's family had moved to a luxury condominium in Fort Lauderdale, Florida. Her father ran a large import-export business. Due to the frequent trips Cuca's parents made to Peru, they opted to send her to an all-girl private boarding school in Florida.

During a school vacation, Cuca – a beach lover— was discovered in her two-piece swimsuit by a major modeling agency. After high school graduation, as a legal young adult – and to the dismay of her parents – she signed her very first modeling contract. She moved to Manhattan, New York to begin her new adult life.

Cuca rented an apartment in Soho; it was her first breath of independence. She brought her childhood pet Hortensia with her. She was a brilliant green and yellow Amazon parrot that her parents had bought her in a farmers market in Peru when Cuca was only six years old. The Indian peasant that sold them the parrot advised Cuca to feed Hortensia with wine-soaked bread to teach her to talk. Hortensia had learned to mimic over 1,000 words, most of them in English, a language the bird had mastered from twelve years in the states. Although she could be funny and entertaining when talking, mimicking American songs or laughing at any little thing, she developed a domineering personality – as did all the females in Cuca's family. When mad, Hortensia's bright green and vibrant yellow feathers would spike. "It's part of her Latin character," Cuca would celebrate in front of her many New York friends. "You should see the way Hortensia reacts when I return late from a photo shoot. She'll fly over my shoulder and yell at me, "Bad girl! Bad girl! Bad girl!"

Cuca although surprised with her spectacular success in modeling, accepted her fame with calm. She responded like a regular person when recognized on the streets. As a highly solicited guest to major social events, she selected the ones to attend very carefully— Cuca had inherited her mother's strong will and moral values, and knew how to avoid conflict or feed the gossip magazines with bad behavior. Her mother frequently flew from Florida to visit her. Both parents had come to accept Cuca's independence, and were proud of her success at work and the way she carried herself.

Everything in Cuca's life was going right. She was involved with a decent young man she dated frequently, who respected her modeling career. Cuca's parents had met him and approved their daughter's selection. She had told her parents that after marrying, she would retire from her modeling career to raise a family.

As fast as success had come to Cuca, a dangerous situation emerged to disturb her otherwise idyllic life. She had noticed a bold, thick-spectacled middle-aged man following her from the moment she stepped on the street. He began to follow her from a watchful distance. When she noticed she was being followed, she would turn and give him a stern look; the man would avoid her eyes, look at the floor as if being ashamed of his behavior, and then would disappear, to reappear again the next day, shortening the distance between them each day.

One day she returned home early to find at the door of her apartment a bouquet of flowers with a card signed "From your fervent admirer". Cuca rushed inside her apartment, locked the door and dialed the police first and right after, a guard dog rental service. A police officer and a guard service representative with a pair of big dogs showed up almost at the same time. Hortensia curiously watched them from her open cage; she seemed intimidated by the dogs.

The police officer wrote out Cuca's complaint and before he left promised to keep in touch with her. The man with the two guard dogs advised her to keep the mastiff dog over the other one. "Although Roofer's massive head makes him look scary, he has a gentle disposition and is good with other pets," the trainer said to her, taking a peek at Hortensia who kept her cautious stand inside her cage.

Cuca soon calmed down her fears with the presence of Roofer in her apartment, and the bodyguard that the modeling agency had provided her. Meantime Hortensia had gotten comfortable with Roofer and began cautiously standing over his head. After a few days she was giving the mastiff orders, "Move! Move!" to which Roofer would obey.

One day upon returning home, Cuca found her apartment door half opened; inside, her stalker had been pinned down by Roofer. He was lying down on the floor, immobilized by the mastiff's paws. Hortensia, standing on the head of the dog, was ordering him, "Bite! Bite! Bite!"

After that incident, Cuca bought Roofer, paying top money for him; she thought it was worthwhile for her safety and for keeping Hortensia and Roofer's platonic friendship going.

9

Brain Change

LEON WAS A CHEERFUL FUN YOUNG KID. He was quite an oddity in a town where the main source of employment was the state prison; famous for its inmate riots and well known criminal residents. Exacerbating the dullness of the town, the spring and summer were short and the winters long, cold, windy and snowy.

Leon and his mother were lucky that his father – a sergeant in the prison – spent most of his time on his job. He seemed always under stress and burned out due to constant threats of prison riots and prison staff absenteeism, which compelled him to work extra overtime hours. Leon and his mother were intimidated by his father's husky body, harsh face and rough demeanor. The patched walls of their home – used as his punching bag – were testimony of his short fuse.

Luckily, Leon had a teacher who encouraged

her students to be inquisitive, creative and unafraid to articulate their opinions. She was a ray of hope in the otherwise gray environment.

"There is nothing that you cannot do within your natural abilities if you make an honest effort," she would cheer her class. "Now, tell me, what would you like to do when you grow up?"

"Leave town," was always the spontaneous answer of the children, to her dismay.

Leon's optimistic early outlook, encouraged by his grammar school teacher, ended by the time he moved through the school system into high school. There, the teachers seemed a mirror reflection of the town mediocrity and indifference. Their negative attitudes and the school's low national test scores always wound up killing the students' dreams of getting a higher education. Leon's mother was devastated when Leon, after barely graduating, decided to become a prison guard. One day, while father and son were working at the prison, she quietly packed a few of her belongings and disappeared from their lives.

Soon after things got worse; a prison riot broke out. The inmates, in an unusually quiet week without major incidents, surprised the guards seizing the prison and taking 60 staff members hostage, among them Leon's father, the hated sergeant who would find any excuse to punish prisoners with solitary confinement. The cell used for solitary was referred as "the hole".

The state began negotiating with the leaders of the revolt. The rioters demanded an end to the prison habit of reclassifying them as "animals" with the sole purpose of treating them as such. Also included was a demand to stop the harassment of the prisoner's families during visiting hours. Forbid the starvation of prisoners sent to "the hole" by feeding them only two tablespoons of food a day – photos of semi-starved inmates getting out of "the hole" confirmed their complaint. They also insisted on training programs that would teach the inmates trades to equip them to face the outside world.

When the horrible uprising was over, 35 guards and 60 prisoners had been killed. The Governor, after accepting most of the prisoner's demands and acknowledging the brutal way the prison had been run, fired the cruel warden and his assistants. He named as his replacement a young capable man highly educated in human relations and prison systems.

The new warden, as soon as he took charge, immediately called a meeting with the prison staff. He expressed his sympathy for all the riot victims – prison staffers and prisoners alike – emphasizing that any human loss regardless of circumstance, should never happen again in the prison.

"I know you're exposed to daily dangerous confrontation with inmates. We are going to retrain you as to how to handle it without need of physical force. You had been working rotating shifts, including weekends and holidays, and you are required to work sometimes additional shifts, resulting in fatigue, low morale and family-related problems. My team is working to correct this situation. From today on, we are going to run group workshops to keep you up-to-date in new techniques to improve the prison environment to benefit you and the inmates."

The enthusiasm and positive leadership of the new warden reminded Leon of his upbeat elementary school teacher. For a short moment he forgot the death of his father at the hands of his capturers. Also, to his surprise, his absent mother had called him to find out how he was doing and let him know she wanted to see him again. He was going to tell her that the new warden, when expressing to him his sympathies for his father's death, had proposed to transfer him to an administrative job with steady daytime work hours.

"I see a lot of potential in you," he had said to him. "Regular men can easily turn to evil when functioning in an environment like the one existing prior to the riot. You never fell into it. With steady normal work hours, you could enroll at college during the evenings. If you do it, I promise to reward you with more promotions."

10

Was It Worth It?

ROGER, IN HIS HIGH SCHOOL SOPHOMORE year became a wide receiver on the football team. His coach wasn't shy about his admiration for him, "He's one of the most naturally gifted players I have ever coached."

Besides being a high prospect for college recruitment – college team scouts were after him – he had a charming personality and superb dancing skills. His mother was a dance instructor. It seemed like the school girls from freshman through senior year all fantasized having him as their sweetheart. Even the teachers loved Roger despite being average academically. After all, with his athletic skills, contagiously happy personality and a possible millionaire future by a pro-team contract, he could afford to be just a mediocre student.

The school was buzzing with excitement; the football team was going to play for a berth in the state semifinals. While walking in the school hallway, Roger crossed paths with the school principal. "We expect a great game from you," the principal greeted him with a big smile and open admiration.

Roger was released from his class early at midday to join his teammates and coach to go over their game strategies. They could hear from the classroom assigned for the pregame meeting the school band and the cheerleaders rehearsing in the stadium.

At 7 p.m. the team ran through the cheerleaders' formed tunnel toward the field while the band exploded with the school song. On the bleachers the parents, students, school staff, and town people all cheered; the fire display went off adding to the carnival noise. Soon after, the game started. There were a few skirmishes at midfield until the quarterback threw Rodger a long pass. He chased it into the touchdown zone. Feeling freed from the defense, he jumped to catch the ball. It was his last recollection from the game. He woke in the hospital with a broken knee that required reconstruction and many sessions of painful therapy. His dream of becoming a professional football player was gone.

Twenty years later, Roger sat nervously on the bleachers, waiting to see his son Kent to play. Memories from his own high school football career burst into his mind. Somehow, the bitterness about his early career ending injury was long gone; his dreams had been rerouted toward his son. Kent wasn't as talented as he was, but he thought with his coaching he may have a chance to be recruited by a college team. He was interrupted from his thoughts by Marlene, his wife.

"I thought you weren't coming," he reacted happily, surprised to see her.

"I overcame my fears," she said. "I want to cheer for Kent."

"He will do fine, don't worry."

Marlene had witnessed the injury that had finished her husband's football career. Even twenty years later, it was fresh in her mind. Then, they were classmates and neighborhood friends. Roger's mother had hired Marlene to help her in her dance studio. During the studio social events, she and Roger enjoyed dancing together. After Roger's injury, his mother asked Marlene to tutor him. Because of the time consumed with the football team, he had fallen behind with his school grades. Marlene became the main reason Roger was able to graduate from high school. It was no surprise when they became engaged and married. Kent was the couple's only child.

Roger's involvement in raising his son, and Marlene's love for them both helped Roger to accept life without football. The only reminder left of his knee injury was a small limp that didn't affect his dancing with his wife.

Since the moment Kent was accepted on the high school team, Marlene had researched the major injuries affecting football players. She was well aware of the effects of a concussion. She had overheard a conversation in her home between Kent and a teammate that reemphasized her fears.

"After I took the hit, I went blank. I found myself off the field without remembering what happened. My coach said I had a concussion and told my parents to take me immediately to the hospital. At the hospital, the doctor explained to my parents that the hard blow to my head had moved the brain rapidly inside my skull. They had to drill a hole in the skull to relieve the swelling pressure."

"Oh, shit, that's scary." Kent had replied.

"Not kidding, dude. The doctor said that fortunately there was no brain bleeding, but it would take five to seven days for my brains to get back to normal."

Roger stood up applauding enthusiastically. Kent, who played as a wide receiver – just as he did 20 years ago – had made a spectacular catch before being tackled out of bounds. The visiting coach had called for a time out. The defense assistant coach furiously jumped over the defensive end player that was supposed to cover Kent.

"God damn it! Why didn't you go to a head to head hit with that kid! You have to scare him!"

Marlene, by nature a sweet lady, overheard his threatening orders. She ran down the bleachers and jumped into the field to face the assistant coach.

"How dare you to tell your player to cause a concussion on my son! What is next, "lay a hat on him" and crush his neck? What kind of trainer are you? Have you seen films of kids coming off of the field paralyzed? You don't deserve to be here; you are either an idiot or a man with criminal instincts!"

Other parents began to circle Marlene and the assistant coach. He was lucky to be rescued from the angered swarm and escorted off the field by three police officers working the game.

Roger never felt more proud of his wife. If somebody like Marlene would have attended the game where he was injured, it may never have happened.

11

Bonded For Trouble

ALVIN PARKED HIS PLUMBING, HEATING and air conditioning service van in the funeral home's parking lot.

"Hi Tim," he walked into the funeral home owner's office. "Any stiffs I know lying in the viewing room?"

"Miss Johnson, the daughter of the judge that sent us to jail. Remember?"

"Oh, yeah, when we got arrested for beating up the illegal Hispanics that were trying to rent apartments in town. We were kids, just graduated from high school. I remember Judge Johnson kept us a week in jail waiting for a trial?"

"Those were the days when you and Burt always got us into trouble…and still do."

"Hey, hey, we are all good buddies, like brothers, like a team. We played football together in high school, enlisted together in the Marines and stuck together when they sent us to fight in 'Nam. After 'Nam we got together again to defend the interest of our town. Not bad!"

"We were lucky that Judge Johnson went easy with us. You guys accepted to enlist in the Marines to avoid going to jail."

"You didn't fare so bad either; he offered to suspend your sentence if you went to college. You became an undertaker while we were risking our asses in 'Nam. But that's another story. Let me fix the heating system before Miss Johnson's viewers freeze inside there," said Alvin walking toward the door.

"Wait," Tim stopped him. "Bert asked me to organize the tailgate party this Sunday. Do you know at what time we'll be leaving?"

"I'll call to let you know," Alvin promised Tim, leaving the office to pick up his tools in the van.

"The 'Seniors Wild Gang' is getting ready to make trouble," the police officer radioed his dispatcher while curiously observing the five buddies loading the SUV and the funeral van with food, spirits and a tent.

"They go early to the Jet's Sunday games at the Meadowlands," the dispatcher replied. "I know them; they are good guys; just sometimes a little crazy."

"They had loaded enough food and drinks to feed the whole stadium," the new town officer replied watching the five friends getting into their vehicles.

The SUV and the van departed for their joy ride to the Meadowlands. In the SUV, Bert, Dan and Jack commented on the humiliating beating the New England Patriots had inflicted on the Jets the previous week. The three were blasting against Mark Sanchez for the interceptions he threw during the game.

"Those bastards forgot how to catch the ball!" Alvin ranted against the Jet's wide receivers, sitting next to Tim in the funeral van. Tim drove, acknowledging him. "How could these bums choose New England to show their weakness? Awful, man! After the game the coach should have cut their balls!"

The SUV and the funeral van went through the stadium's gate and parked side to side in their usual parking spot, and set up the long tent. Under the tent's shelter they started the grill. Soon the smell of the steaks, hamburgers, sausages and pieces of chicken sizzling over the flames spread through the air. The five buddies gathered around the grill's heat; it was a cold Sunday. They sipped beers and drank shots of Jack Daniels. By then they had forgotten about the Jets' fiasco the past week and were remembering the town's beauties; the ones that had married common friends and those that had moved out of town. They started attacking the food while trying to decide which of the beauties had the best bosom.

The parking lot was beginning to slowly fill with other tailgating fans. A few parking spaces down, a group began to throw a football. Three young Hispanic men playing as wide receivers chased the ball toward the spot where the "Seniors Wild Gang" was eating drinking and laughing, feeling young again. After a few throws, one of the wide receivers accidentally tipped the ball over the gang's loaded grill. The steaks, hamburgers, sausages and chicken flew up and landed all over the pavement.

"S.O.B!" Alvin grabbed the ball and with a large kitchen knife began to pierce it.

"I'm going to beat the shit out you!" Bert charged one of the young Mexicans. The two other wide receivers ran to protect and help their friend, immobilizing Bert. Dan, by nature the quietest of the five friends, driven by his old marine instinct ran to free Bert.

"Come on, guys! Let's cool it!" Jack with his skills for diplomacy, stopped Alvin who after stabbing the ball to pieces tried to attack with the knife the group that held hostage Dan and Bert.

"Yeah, guys, let's all cool it," a young Hispanic man, part of the football playing group, in perfect English, approached Tim and shook hands with him. Tim had cautiously stayed away from the warriors. "We know we have caused damage to your property and spoiled your party. We brought plenty of food with us. We can share it and pray that Mark Sanchez doesn't screw up this time," he laughed breaking the angry silence of the group.

Jack, freeing Alvin, approached the young Mexican appeaser and also shook hands with him. "You got a deal; we accept your invitation to tacos, burritos and to chug-a-lug of Corona."

"You guys can share our booze," volunteered Alvin, calming down. "You look like decent guys."

The three wide receivers freed Bert and Dan. It was time to taste Mexican food and keep drinking.

12

Elvis and Me

THE STREETS WERE DESERTED; THE COLD and windy night had kept the people inside. A dog was scavenging for food, stopping and raising his front paws over the garbage can rims to sink his nose inside, then continuing on with his patrol if he didn't find any leftovers. After trotting several blocks, he approached the huge hole where the Twin Towers once stood. At the Fire House corner, he turned into Trinity Place. He struck luck in front of a Chinese restaurant; at its curbside were the barrels with the day's food disposal. He knocked down one barrel and chewed fiercely the half- eaten pork ribs and pieces of chicken remains that spilled out of it, even eating most of the softer small bones. His belly finally filled, he began searching for a warm place to lie down.

Chester was enjoying the best winter of his homeless life in a quiet, safe and warm refuge. Next to his improvised cardboard bed lay a half-empty bottle of cheap wine, his stringless guitar and two plastic garbage bags filled with street-collectibles.

Weeks ago, he had found in the Meatpacking District a meat locker hook used to hang the carcasses in the freezers. He hid it inside his pants; it would help him to defend himself against the crazy homeless that sometimes showed up at Trinity Place to try to claim his territory.

Chester's daily morning work routine consisted of standing in front of the employee entrance to The American Stock Exchange. He would stand with his stringless guitar simulating the playing of a rock tune while singing it with his gravelly, ragged voice. The traders liked him and rewarded his "air guitar" street show with generous tips. One morning, as he finished his concert, he noticed, one block away, two Electric Company workers coming out of their truck. They removed the cast iron lid that covered the manhole from which a rich steam escaped to the street. To pry open the manhole lid, they used a hook similar to the one Chester had found.

That night he waited for the stores to close and the office cleaning crews to finish their tasks and leave the area. Alone on the street, Chester walked to the manhole and using his hook tried to open it. After a short struggle, he removed the lid enough to squeeze in. Standing on the built-in metal ladder, he closed the manhole from inside; then, lighting his way with matches, found along the electrical cables a place to sleep. Once he settled in, he traced the steam that escaped to the street from the basement of the building in front of the manhole. He felt lucky to have found a rent- free, safe and well heated place to call home.

His sympathizers at the American Stock Exchange, before leaving for that long weekend, had given him generous tips to buy food. Among them there were a few younger traders that remembered when Chester played for an upcoming rock band that had an enthusiastic following and a bright future. Unfortunately, drugs and alcohol had destroyed the group's dreams.

Chester, instead of buying food, bought six bottles of cheap Night Train wine. He was planning to hide himself in the warm manhole and drink the weekend away. He was sound asleep under the effect of the wine when a strong barking from the street awoke him. Climbing the metal stairs, he cursed at the dog and knocked on the manhole cover with the hook to try to scare him away. The dog persisted with his barking and compelled Chester to open the lid to chase him away. As soon as he opened the lid, the dog jumped in, landing on Chester's chest and knocking him off the stairs. Chester lay unconscious on the manhole floor. As he regained his senses, he noticed the morning light filtering into the hole; and worse, a smelly snoring dog sleeping over him. He tried to free himself from the dog, but the dog started to wag his tail and lick his face with no intention of moving.

"What the hell are you doing here?" He tried to push him away.

The dog, encouraged by Chester's attention,

intensified his licking.

Back from the long weekend, Chester's sympathizers at the American Stock Exchange were surprised to find him in the company of the Jack Russell terrier mix. The dog seemed to enjoy Chester's morning concerts, lying at his feet, next to the hat were the tips were deposited. "Hey Chester, what is the dog's name?" one of the traders asked him.

"Elvis…In honor of my idol, man."

Chester and Elvis soon became a fixture in Trinity Place. When Chester would get drunk and lie asleep on the sidewalk, Elvis would bark aggressively at anyone trying to get close to them. The dog had become Chester's loyal guardian. There was only one young trader from the American Stock Exchange, Sam, whom the dog would allow to touch Chester. Every morning Sam brought dog food and treats for Elvis and petted him.

It was Sam who noticed how Chester's mental condition had been deteriorating. The years of alcohol and drug abuse, exacerbated by his harsh homeless life, had caught up with him. Sam arranged for an ambulance to take Chester to be treated for dementia. That same day Sam brought Elvis to his home as his borrowed pet, planning to keep him for as long as it was needed ...maybe forever

.

13

A Brooklyn Blink

BYRON AND DINAH, IN THEIR EARLY thirty's, were expecting their second and last child in their meticulously structured life. They lived in a tranquil cul-de-sac in Basking Ridge, New Jersey. Their home was modern, spacious, and full of light and happiness. It was their oasis of privacy and relaxation.

Both with roots in Brooklyn, New York, came from lower middle class familics. They had graduated from college paid with scholarships and student loans. Their careers had opened the doors to well-paying jobs and bright futures; they were living the American dream in an affluent town.

The birth of their second child was a month away. Dinah was in the middle of changing jobs, expecting the arrival of their baby before moving to her new employment. Everything was going along smoothly until, unexpectedly, Byron's firm went into bankruptcy. Besides losing his job, his retirement fund – fully invested in the firm's stocks – went up into smoke.

"What will happen now?" Dinah worried. "I won't be able to work for two months after the baby is born. Meantime we'll have to pay our mortgage and the baby will bring extra expenses. In addition, we are paying the highest average property taxes in the nation. If that isn't bad enough, we also face the monthly payments for the new family van we just bought, and the student loans still lingering seven years after we graduated."

"I'll find a job soon; with my experience it shouldn't be any problem," Byron tried to calm his wife. "Remember all the job offers I received from other companies tempting me with higher salaries?"

Byron, without time to recover from the shock of losing his job and retirement funds, began searching for a new job. To his surprise, the companies that had tried to attract him with higher salaries were not hiring. The country had entered into a severe economic crisis, dragging down many families like his.

The birth of their second child brought a momentarily distraction to the couple's monetary troubles. Byron begged Dinah to just worry about the children and leave him in charge of paying the bills. He hadn't yet told her that the third quarter property tax was delinquent and their bank savings after a couple months of being unemployed were gone. The unemployment check he received barely covered food, heat and electric bills. When he realized they eventually would be evicted from their home, he decided to put the house up for sale expecting to get back part of its equity. With the money from the sales, they could afford a more modest house. The real estate agent that had sold them the house told Byron his home in the current market had lost at least one third of its valuc. It was worthless to sell it; he wouldn't recover a penny from the original investment. The only way out of the finance mess was to keep looking for work, even at a much lower pay. Meantime he started charging on his credit cards, a forbidden rule for them.

During a break from the long hours he spent on his laptop sending job applications, he searched the internet about the effect it would have his unpaid property tax bill. To his dismay, he learned that it would be optioned as a tax lien, creating a potential gold mine for the buyer. If not paid in time with additional high interest charges included, the owner of the lien could opt for foreclosure, evict his family, and take possession of their home for pennies on the dollar.

That Friday, Byron went to the supermarket and spent more than what his strict budget permitted. His parents were coming to see the baby. He did not tell them about the loss of his job. Dinah and he had decided not to involve their families with their monetary struggles. He already had decided to completely stop the mortgage and property tax payments. The real estate agent had explained to him that the mortgage bank would be forced to buy the delinquent liens from the investor who got it at the town auction, and then proceed to foreclose and evict his family, a process which would take approximately two years. By then Byron expected to be working and able to rent a home.

His parents were excited to see the baby. Byron's mother and Dinah stayed with the older child and the baby while Byron and his father went to watch a football game in the family recreation room.

"I learned a few days ago about the bankruptcy of your company," his father accepted the beer from Byron. "Are you still working?"

"We're okay Dad, don't worry."

"That tells me you're not working. Besides seeing the baby I came to let you know that you, Dinah and the children will always be welcome to live with us."

"We don't want to burden you and mom with our problems."

"Son, your problem is transitory. You can lose your job, your home, but nobody can take away your education. You guys are young, educated and smart. We'll be happy to have all of you living with us. When things improve you will find a better job than the one you lost. Meantime, your mom and I think it will be good for you to return to your roots in Brooklyn."

"Thank you Dad. I'm lucky to have you and mom as my parents."

14

My Filthy Rich Brother

THE TWO BROTHERS COULDN'T HAVE BEEN more different. Ernest was outspoken, charming, manipulative, and extremely ambitious – which he sugar-coated with his vibrant personality. He was the younger of the two. Chris, the older one, was quiet and reserved; a generous soul always willing to help others.

Their traits followed the brothers into maturity. Chris became an accountant, married his high school sweetheart, and lived a peaceful life. The couple's main goal was to raise their three sons to be honest, useful citizens. Chris was always attentive to the needs of his wife, Shirley, their sons, and aging parents. He and Shirley lived within the comfort of their middle class income, which they administered in a prudent way.

Ernest studied law, and while preparing for his degree, involved himself in local politics. After receiving his law degree, he married the daughter of a powerful state politician who was thrilled by his new son-in-law's political ambitions and smartness. He gave Ernest his full support during his senatorial campaign. During the primaries, Ernest used Machiavellian tactics against his two opponents. His running mates, seasoned politicians more qualified than him, would never forget his dirty election tricks. Fortunately, his constituents only saw the young, charismatic candidate full of fresh ideas and enthusiasm. They backed him in the primaries and general election, choosing him as their new state senator.

A couple years later, Ernest, with his eyes set on Washington, – along with the unconditional support of his father-in-law – ran for a seat in the House of Representatives. As a state senator he had been active giving speeches in his district and making himself visible on local TV. He always supported popular causes, not by conviction, but for his own political interest and gain. It paid handily; he was sent as one of the new rising stars to Washington, where he quickly won the trust and backing of his party leader.

After the initial excitement for his political success began to wear down – and the boredom of having to attend long committee sessions that usually went nowhere – his interest shifted toward the Congressional after hours social life. Washington was a fascinating town, especially for a young married congressman living alone. He began dating lonely secretaries from the Capitol Building and attended parties organized by Washington lobbyist groups sending contributions towards his reelection campaign.

During Congressional recesses, the lobby groups invited him to travel to exotic places overseas, which he accepted under the guise of securing new export markets for his state. After his third reelection – and completion of his five years of public service he needed to qualify for retirement and medical benefits – Ernest resigned from his seat in Congress to accept a lucrative contract from a major lobbyist firm. His connections with the powerful committee chairman's in Congress began to produce benefits. He wasn't surprised by the welcome he received from the lobby firm's president, "It's nice to have you aboard. You made the right decision coming to work with us; Congress doesn't make the laws, we do."

Chris and Shirley's well planned life allowed them to easily provide for their three sons college education expenses. One of their sons was close to graduation, and the other two, a few years behind.

"When the boys finish college I'm going to take an early retirement and we'll travel around the world to all the places we've always dreamed of visiting," Chris said to his wife. As their sons grew up, Shirley obtained a real estate license. She – now a realtor – had begun to work part-time in the middle of the housing boom, helping to add to the couple's savings.

That Monday Chris drove to his job, happily singing along with the car radio, excited by the prospects of a future life as a retiree. As soon as he arrived, he noticed his coworkers were distressed. "What's going on?" he asked one of his subordinates from accounting.

"The company has declared bankruptcy," was his shocking answer. "Our acquisitions with borrowed money, and the internal disorganization finally caught up with us."

Chris had sensed from his branch office the irrational behavior the founder and CEO of his company kept by acquiring and merging larger corporations to theirs, increasing the debt of his now giant conglomerate to dangerous levels. Yet, Wall Street, with each acquisition, had rewarded their company's stock by increasing its value.

"How could that S.O.B tell us on last Friday's phone conference that our corporation was going to surprise Wall Street with spectacular quarterly gains," sobbed another employee.

Company rules only allowed them to acquire shares of their company for their Individual Retirement Accounts, and could only sell the shares if retiring or leaving the job.

Chris saw his major life savings go up in smoke. But there was more misery to follow; during the corporate bankruptcy and reorganization he lost his job.

How could we be in this situation? Shirley's wondered as she and Chris packed to move to a small apartment. They had just sold their home to continue financing their sons' college expenses. Shirley's recent real estate career had come to a screeching halt with the collapse of the housing market. She was working a part-time job as a secretary while Chris had accepted a job making half his former salary. Shirley thought about Ernest; her brother-in-law who had become filthy rich as a successful lobbyist in Washington. We have turned into a dysfunctional country where bullshit artists quickly become wealthy while honest workers are sacrificed by the system, she realized bitterly.

15

Sunshine A La Carte

SETH AND VERA CELEBRATED THEIR 25TH wedding anniversary flying to a Puerto Plata's resort, in the Dominican Republic. As the plane descended into Puerto Plata, they admired the clear sea and its sandy bottom.

"We'll have a great vacation," Seth said as he kissed his wife.

The resort's bus picked them up, together with a dozen of the other jet passengers. After unpacking, Seth and Vera decided to take a dip in the pool before going for dinner. When they approached the huge pool, Vera pointed at one of the sun bathers, "She is naked!" Noting Seth's instant interest in the woman, she scolded him. "Don't stare at her with that lascivious look! If you keep that up, I'm going to take off my suit top. I'm better looking than her!"

"Believe me, dear, it is not lust, it is just

curiosity. There are a lot of European tourists coming to this resort bringing with them their topless culture."

"That woman is not topless; she is nude!"

As they got closer, they realized that the tan-colored bottom of the woman's suit made her appear naked, but she was only topless. And she wasn't alone; in the pool a group of topless women were playing volleyball with a group of men.

To Seth's surprise, Vera took off her top and jumped into the pool. "Put it back on!" he protested. His wife smiled and ignored him. Seconds later, Seth – over his initial annoyance – accepted the invitation for him to join in the volleyball game.

"I'm going to go to the resort's shop to buy a thong bathing suit like the ones the guys playing volleyball wore," said Seth, still uncomfortable and resentful of his wife's new display of boldness and defiance.

"You sound jealous."

"I'm upset but not jealous."

"I want a G-string too, like the ones the girls playing volleyball wore. For the first time in my life I'm beginning to feel liberated."

Back from vacation, Vera was surprised to see Seth searching for nudist camps on his laptop. "Are you serious about it?" she asked him. "I thought vacation was over and we were back to our traditional life style."

"I felt great in my G-string with the freedom of walking on the beach and getting almost a full sun tan. It was stress-relieving. I want to repeat that experience, but now totally naked. Would you join me?"

"I don't know … Does New Jersey have nudist camps?"

"There is one near us."

"What would happen if we met some of our neighbors there?"

"The nudist resorts claim their members come from every walk of life that includes our neighbors too."

"Okay, we'll give it a try." Vera stood silent for a moment and then burst into a laugh, "It must be hard to guess the poor from the wealthy when everybody walks around naked; it becomes a kind of equalizer."

The couple, in the beginning of a rebellion against their middle-class principals, attended the pre-acceptance screening given to the nudist camp postulants: "We are not a swingers club; this is a social family experience. Our moral codes bar members that make disparaging comments about another member's body or physical appearance. Another mandate we enforce is that members should always look one another in the eyes – engaging in roving gazes and prolonged staring upon one another's anatomy is cause for permanent removal from the club."

The woman instructor looked with a sweet smile at the six couples and two families with children attending the screening. "To prove whether you are ready to become members of our camp, we'll start undressing." She calmly took off her blouse and observed the group doing it.

"We are saving a fortune in clothes since we became nudist," Seth, sitting in front of his laptop, said to Vera in the kitchen. Both were fully naked. She was baking cookies for the costumed trick or treaters that would be arriving soon.

The doorbell rang. She picked up a tray with cookies and went to open the door. Seth from his desk, still at his laptop, heard the loud Ooooh! He realized Vera had forgotten to cover herself. He ran to pull his naked wife into the house. A new strident Ooooh! was heard when Seth tripped on Vera and fell over her on the walkway. As the parents rushed to pull their children away from the grotesque view of two naked adults awkwardly wrestling, an older kid in a skeleton costume sneaked around the couple and closed the door, locking them out.

A couple weeks later Seth mailed the payment imposed on them by the judge for indecent exposure. A for sale sign hung outside their home; Vera, too ashamed from the Halloween incident, had begged Seth to sell their home and move to a faraway neighborhood, but not too far from the nudist club.

16

The Ballad Singer

ARTURO HAD ONLY ONE TALENT IN LIFE TO dream of, one that demanded excellence, youth or just plain luck. He was pretty good at it, but not enough to get a decent shot at success. His middle age and lack of formal education could have been a detriment in his work life, but not for him; he had no responsibilities and was worry free. He excelled as a self-taught guitar player, singer and composer. He played in local bars for tips and neighborhood family parties for a low fee, drinks and food. He promoted himself as 'a voice and a guitar to lift the soul'.

Arturo flourished when performing; it seemed to vaporize away his few pressures. He had separated from his wife after many bitter fights caused by his affairs. His wife – because of religious beliefs – had opposed their divorce but was relieved to live apart from him. At the present, he lived with Carole, his mistress, in a tiny apartment.

"This is better than a large home; it keeps us close," he would say to her. Carole took care of his clothes, cooked for him and financially carried most of their home expenses. She was a secretary making a decent income, but had the misfortune to fall in love with an unreliable man. The first time she met Arturo was at a party where the hired charming ballad singer flirted and dedicated several of his romantic compositions to Carole. She felt struck by Cupid's arrow even before the first song ended. She agreed to live with him; her life had been until then a lonely one, but her strong feelings for this singing Romeo eased her aloneness.

When Arturo returned home at early morning hours, he would slide quietly into bed and curl his body to Carole's. Her body always made him feels he was embracing his precious guitar. He would awake at 10 in the morning; by that time Carole had long left for her secretarial job. He would take a quick shower and go to his other job, the one that supplemented his irregularly scheduled evening gigs.

Arturo's second job was as a fast cook during lunch hours at a coffee shop grill. He wasn't bad at the grill. He developed a unique way to use the spatula entertainingly flipping the burgers, omelets, steaks, sausages and home fries. He would also use the spatula handle as a drum stick to hit the stainless grill top and create great percussion beats, staging quite a side show to the delight of the customers seated at the counter. He would now and then find a way to pinch the flirty waitresses while throwing the spatula into the air; they would laugh at it – he was such a charming guy. The owners of the coffee shop, two brothers, also liked Arturo, but couldn't understand why when they tried to pinch the waitresses they would always resent it.

Arturo's free spirited life came to a halt when a terse call from his grown up son, Arthur Jr., notified him of his wife's demise. He then realized she had been a noble faithful wife. His wife single handed had raised their two children; Arthur Jr., a high school teacher and Rose a nurse. Both of them resented him for the pain he had caused their mother and for failing them as a father. I have been a lucky man, Arturo thought. The two women I loved most in my life have truly loved me.

Arturo attended the funeral service and accompanied his wife's coffin to the cemetery. His two children just ignored him. It was a long chilly moment that made him for the first time feel ashamed of himself. He left the graveyard burdened with grief and guilt.

Out of respect for her death, he discontinued for a time his musical activities. After his job at the coffee shop, he would rush back home ignoring the waitresses' flirtations. His new "devoted husband" life helped him to better appreciate Carole's unselfish dedication to him. Carole, noticing his sudden change, enjoyed for the first time with him a normal home life.

When Arturo felt ready to restart his presentation at the bars, Carole's health began to deteriorate. She passed away shortly after. It impacted Arturo, both, emotionally and economically – he had no money to bury her.

Arturo's children didn't have time in their busy lives to visit their mother's grave. A few months after her funeral, Arthur Jr. paid his first visit to her. He was surprised out of his socks to find his mother's tomb being shared with another woman. Infuriated, he ran to the cemetery office. His sister and he had fully paid for her resting place, not to be violated or shared by a stranger!

"Your father brought Carole's body to be buried next to your mother," the cemetery administrator showed him the cemetery's log. "As your mother's husband he was legally entitled to do it."

After a heated argument with the administrator, Arthur Jr. stomped out of the cemetery promising to fight it out in court.

The secretary of the cemetery administrator approached her boss, "The father of that young man is a very charming person with a beautiful voice. He is the one that comes with his guitar to sing to his two ladies; with his songs he attracts the cemetery's visitors. He composed and recorded for the two of them the song, 'The Two Loves of my Life', a big hit now being played in all the radio stations."

17

Joe's Problem

JOE COULD HAVE BEEN THE POSTER CHILD of a lower middle-class young American. Physically, culturally, and economically he was a perfect fit. He made his living as a supervisor at an international shipping company. Joe's fluent knowledge of Spanish had helped him supervise his workers to load and unload the containers. His easy going personality had made him popular with his crew. Also, the Spanish workers had not forgotten when a few days ago Immigration Agents had unexpectedly showed up at the loading yard. Joe had run to tip off the ones inside the warehouse to hide, limiting the numbers of illegal workers arrested just to the five men that were in the yard at the time. The illegal men still working in the company after the Immigration raid came to realize that Joe, besides being an easy going friendly guy – who could turn into a strict boss if needed – was also kind and compassionate.

Joe's blue-collar neighborhood completed his universe. He lived there with his aging parents, and was surrounded by his childhood friends. They had been his classmates from pre-kindergarten to senior year of high school. They were also teammates on the school's football and baseball teams. As grownups, the group was bonded by solid long time friendships. On weekends they would carry beer and food to gather at a friend's home who his turn was to host it. They would drink, eat, watch sports, remember anecdotes from the past, talk about their jobs, dream about possible business ventures (that seldom materialized), remember ex-girlfriends, pals who had married and left the neighborhood, and the few, who for lack of decent paying jobs, had enlisted in the Armed Forces. Joe was going to be one of them, but before he signed on, the job offer came in from the international shipping company. His Spanish background saved him from going to fight in Afghanistan.

Joe learned Spanish from his parents. They didn't tell him the country they came from – they both claimed to have been born in the USA. "We're proud citizens of this country; that's all you have to know," was always their answer. When alone, his parents spoke fluent Spanish between themselves, and demanded Joe learns it. "It would help you to get a better job in the future," was their reasoning. They wound up being so right!

His parents' English was fluid but with a

slight accent – they always consulted Joe when in doubt with their pronunciation. It had become an ongoing obsession to speak English like a native born American. In spite of it, because of their light accent, the neighborhood thought they were European immigrants. Joe had his father's features – blond, blue eyes, white skin, and tall; he felt as American as an apple pie.

That morning Joe opened the company yard early to check the loaded containers to be taken to the pier for shipping overseas. One of his workers also showed up early and introduced him to his cousin.

"He wants job, mi primo good worker."

"Does he have his green card and social security?" Joe asked his worker, knowing full well that most of them had bogus documentation. In the company office they didn't care; they just wanted to have copy of something that looked legal to protect themselves against heavy fines for hiring illegal workers.

The rest of his crew showed up a little later and began loading other containers. A couple hours after Joe was paged to the front office. There were two Immigration officers waiting for him. He thought right away it had to do with the illegal worker they had hired that morning. He was wrong – they came looking for him, accusing Joe of being an illegal worker!

At the immigration offices Joe insisted he was an American born citizen – his whole neighborhood could testify for him.

"Listen Joe, we're not fools. We noticed the other day when you ran inside the warehouse to alert the other illegal's to hide. That motivated us to check your background. Look what we found," the immigration agent handed him a copy of their evidence.

Joe read: "Fifteen years ago, his middle-age parents, with their two year old son, traveled from Colombia using tourist visas. Their tourist visitation permit expired, but by then they had disappeared among the millions of illegal immigrants in USA. Since Joe's father was born in Colombia from a European immigrant family, his features helped him and his wife to blend with the local population without raising suspicions. They choose California as their residence. Joe's father, a shrewd man, found out a family of three – husband, wife and a child – from a newspaper article, believed dead after a fire had burned their home to the ground. After getting their names and birth dates, he had paid a few dollars for replacement copies of their birth certificates at the local county clerk's office. Then Joe's father moved with his family to New Jersey, where using the birth certificates as identification, obtained a driver license and later a copy of what he claimed was his lost Social Security card".

"So, wise ass, you and your parents will be sent to jail while waiting for extradition," said the Immigration officers. Joe was stunned, in total disbelief, still trying to absorb this total redraft of his life.

"Do you want to know how we discovered

your father's fraud?" the other officer asked Joe. Joe was too much in shock to respond, but that didn't stop the agent, "The child of the burned family was at his grandparent's home the day of the fire. Now he is complaining to the Internal Revenue Service of being taxed for unknown incomes."

Joe's parent's fraud triggered a massive controversy in the national media. Should children of illegal immigrants be penalized for their parent's actions? Should Joe be treated as an accomplice and held accountable for his employer's policy of 'overlooking' bogus documentation? After lengthy, heated court debates, Joe was permitted to apply for permanent residence. His parents, due to their advanced ages, were charged with fraud, and ordered to serve life sentences at their home, which allowed them to avoid deportation.

18

What An Amazing Business!

A JOB DIGNIFIES THE PERSON WHO DOES IT, reasoned Jonathan. It doesn't matter what impact the job has on society – that's for others to judge.

Jonathan walked happily toward the train station. Days ago he had bought a book written by two holistic physicians advising workers how to deal with bosses they couldn't stand. His brother-in-law, who always had complained about the controlling, know-it-all, aggressive bosses he had to put up with on a daily basis, gracefully accepted the book as a gift from him. "Thank you, maybe this book will teach me how to deal with those bastards. By the way, in all these years we have known each other; I have never heard you complain about your job or your bosses. It's funny; I don't have a clue as to what you do for a living. What exactly is your job?"

"I'm a kind of businessman," Jonathan explained to him.

"What kind of business are you in?"

"I'm sorry, but the nature of my work required me to sign a confidentiality agreement and I cannot discuss it."

"Are you in an illegal business?"

"Do I look like a crook to you?"

"Not really. As matter of fact you always strike me as a college professor or an intellectual. The glasses you wear, the way you dress, the leather briefcase you always carry…You look very respectful."

"I have to dress up for my job," Jonathan said with a sense of modesty.

"Is your three miles jogging daily part of it? Do you do it to run from your bosses or the police?"

"Now you're getting funny," laughed Jonathan. "Just read the book; it may help you to end your miseries at work."

That morning, on his way to the train station, Jonathan stopped to buy the Wall Street Journal. At the station, he walked down the stairs to the track where his train stops. As he expected, the train was not too crowded. He got a seat and opened the newspaper to glance at it. He had a business registered under the name of his wife and their two older sons. It was a company that invested mainly in rental properties in Florida, only leaving a small percentage of it to speculate in the stock market. The properties' income was producing enough for his retirement; but he needed to keep doing his job just as a fish needed water to survive. It pumped his adrenaline and made him feel useful. Without it, boredom would ruin his mental and physical health.

Jonathan got off at Times Square to transfer to another train that stopped at Wall Street. As he expected, a larger crowd was waiting for it. He blended among a group of people dressing conservatively and looking prosperous. When the train came and the waiting crowd rushed into it, he got in the middle of the pack. As the doors closed, he slowly squeezed through the passengers toward the door at the center of the car. When the door opened on the next station he got out – once more his sticky fingers had done the job. Inside his briefcase were three wallets!

He sat on a train station bench and without taking the wallets out of the briefcase, pulled the money from them. He proceeded to pack each one of the wallets inside the briefcase in different paper bags. He got off the train station and threw one paper bag into a street garbage basket. After walking a few blocks more he had gotten rid of the other two. It was his way to avoid knowing the identity of his victims and feeling guilty.

He took a taxi to midtown, where he had an early lunch and finished reading The Wall Street Journal. Before leaving, he called the broker in charge of his family funds and made a trade.

It was time for him to hit Lexington, Madison and Fifth Avenues. He would lift cash from the purses of wealthy women or tourists, usually when they crowded in a corner waiting for the lights to change and cross the streets.

Today had been very productive. I need three more hits and I'm done for the day, he planned. He got his next two victims on the corner of St. Patrick Cathedral. One more and I'll go home, he reminded himself; tomorrow I'll work the airports. His strategy was to never come back during the week to the same place; caution, caution, caution was his main motto.

When he was on his third hit, trying to lift money from a plain clothed police woman's unzipped purse, he was quickly surrounded by three policemen. It happened so fast; he didn't have time to put to use his daily three miles training.

Jonathan' wife and their two older sons were loading a rental truck to move to one of their properties in Florida. They didn't know that Jonathan was a pickpocket and were still in shock. Before his arrest, Jonathan had told her he had had problems with the IRS. Since their investment was under her and their two sons names, he was going to divorce her to completely disassociate himself from his family's wealth. This way justice could not touch their fortune. His wife realized that Jonathan was a crook, but also a very shrewd person and a loyal family man. "We'll be in Florida waiting for him to serve his sentence," she had said to their two sons.

19

I Found You!

NELSON HAD HEARD THAT WHEN PEOPLE are near death their important moments in life flash back in their minds. He knew he had reached that time. He was a terminal cancer patient marking time in what he perceived the final countdown of his existence.

He was just an ordinary man with no worthwhile accomplishments. His most important moment of life had happened when Deborah became his high-school sweetheart. A smile spread across his face.

"Hi," he was half awake from his stupor. "It's nice to see you smiling today," the nurse wiped a cool cloth across Nelson's sweating face. Terry couldn't tell whether the patient heard her or not. She lifted his arm to inject him with a new dose of morphine to calm down his stomach pain. She held his hands briefly before leaving to check on the other patients. Nelson tried to follow the nurse with his eyes, but the quick effect of the morphine knocked him semiconscious again.

Terry wondered why she felt so attracted to Nelson. He was just another terminally-ill patient in her unit. Outside her hospital job, she lived a happy married life as the mother of three children. Terry had grown up fatherless. She and her younger sister, in their conversations as teenagers, wondered why there were no photos of their father in their home; but they always respected their mother's privacy, which prevailed over their curiosity.

Nelson's thoughts transported him to the time when Deborah told him she was pregnant. They both had just graduated from high school. He had found a job as a bank mailroom clerk. They hurried to get married in a private ceremony under the sour disapproval of Deborah's parents – especially her mother, who wanted her to have an abortion and break up with him.

Since Nelson's salary couldn't support the young couple to rent their own place, they moved temporarily into Deborah's parent's home. He was an easy going guy to get along with. In a polite way, he ignored Deborah's parents open criticism about him and his humble upbringing. Her mother soon took full control of her granddaughter, isolating Deborah and him from their baby; she was an extremely possessive woman.

A few months after giving birth to her daughter, to the dismay of her family, Deborah got pregnant again and had another baby girl. At that time Nelson's bank merged with another institution and his job was eliminated. Unemployed, he became a bigger target for his vicious mother-in-law's criticism, to the point that it was impossible for him to continue living under the same roof with her.

"I love you and our daughters more than my life," he told Deborah. "I'm going back to school in the evenings and I will keep looking for work. I'll come back for you and our daughters as soon as I can afford a place to live."

He moved to his parent's tiny apartment, and then accepted a job out of state. As soon as he relocated, he tried phoning Deborah to give her his new address, but her family had changed their number. Then he wrote letters to her that were returned to him by the post office stamped, "Wrong Address". When he had saved enough, he came back for his wife and the girls only to find out that her family had moved.

Terry fully enjoyed the weekend with her husband and three children. She loved the warm family atmosphere they had created to raise them. It became her major goal in life to give her children the support she never had; a father at home.

That Monday morning, when Terry returned to her job in the hospital, the head nurse approached her. She had noticed the special care and extra time Terry had for the patient with stomach cancer. As gentle as she could, she said to her, "The patient that you cared so much about passed away yesterday. He left on his bed table an envelope. I opened the manila envelope and found letters stamped "wrong address". The hospital authorized us to go through his mail. Would you like to read them?"

Terry, overcome by an inexplicable emotion toward the deceased patient, opened and read the old letters that her father had tried to send to her mother. The head nurse and her coworkers – as they learned the reason for her emotional outburst – tried to console her.

"I believed my mother loved my father until the day she died; she never remarried," said Terry to her coworkers trying to control her emotions. "My sister's family and mine are going to give him a dignified funeral. He will not go to his resting place alone, we'll be there showing him our love."

20

Wildlife Keeper

MARVIN'S PARENTS OWNED A DAIRY FARM in Wisconsin where his childhood responsibilities – when he was not in school – were to help Jose to milk and feed the cows. The old Mexican worker used to pet and talk to the cows. The animals responded to Jose with loud moos. Soon Marvin began petting and talking to the cows and they would moo back at him.

Marvin's love for animals motivated him to graduate from college as a Wildlife Biologist. He was hired by the World Wildlife Foundation to work in South Africa and became, at a young age, a well-respected professional. Zoos worldwide began contacting him when in need of new species. He would accept orders from zoos that qualified with proper habitat facilities. He was a strong advocate against sending to zoos animals captured in their native habitat. Once convinced the animals would enjoy a comfortable captive life, he would send the zoos species grown or rehabilitated in sanctuary farms. These animals couldn't be reintegrated to wildlife.

The World Wildlife Foundation offered Marvin the opportunity to run the largest sanctuary farm in Africa. The farm cared and rehabilitated all kind of species and provided bungalows to host teams of wildlife experts. The teams besides their work duties in the farm advised Africans and trained them to be wildlife rangers. The farm had large ponds, tall grass areas and a forest; it was an oasis in the otherwise arid surroundings.

Marvin lived alone in his bungalow. Although he felt fulfilled by his job, he lamented the lack of opportunities to meet young women. Fortunately, through a friend, he met Margaret, the daughter of a wealthy South African family with roots in England. She was attending medical school in London and was in her last year, still undecided whether to stay in England or return to South Africa after graduation.

That day Marvin had ordered his maid to make the bungalow look spic-and-span. At evening Margaret was coming to pay him her first visit. She was interested in seeing if their professional careers wouldn't interfere with their desire to have a happy marriage.

When Margaret stopped her SUV in front of Marvin's bungalow, he came out to welcome her. He led her to the bungalow's dining room. The maid and her husband, dressed in elegant waiter and waitress outfits could have caused the envy of any English valet. They stood quietly in a corner of the dining room, waiting Marvin's orders.

After Marvin helped Margaret to her chair and sat at the head of the table, he ordered the champagne to be served. The background of a sweet melody accompanied their toasts. The dinner, ordered from a well-known restaurant, was consumed amid Margaret's anecdotes of her medical studies in England. She seemed at ease, spiked by the drinks and happy to be with Marvin.

After dinner Marvin asked her to wait for him on the front porch for a surprise American dessert. As she walked to the front porch, Marvin tipped the maid and her husband generously. Both disappeared out the back porch door.

As Marvin was preparing a tray with tea and cheesecake – flown to him from the states – a loud scream made him leave the dessert tray and run to the front porch. When he heard a second scream he crashed through the darkened screen door and landed on top of the huge blubbery body of Precious. She rolled her eyes upward looking at him with her semi-sleepy eyes, without moving.

In the shadow of the night, Marvin saw Kent – his bungalow neighbor, near Margaret's SUV. Kent and his wife were the farm reptile experts.

Kent's wife approached Marvin, "When your friend walked onto the porch, Precious was asleep on it. Your guest got scared and screamed. Surprised, Precious stood up, which startled your guest into a panic by her enormous size. Your guest dash for refuge in her car."

"My wife and I were on our porch when she screamed and ran to her SUV, said Kent with a strong voice. "I went to her and tried to calm her down. I explained to her that the baby hippopotamus was your pet and was harmless, but your friend screamed again and fainted."

As Marvin walked in the shadow and approached the SUV, he saw Kent better. He had rolled over and around his neck and shoulders his favorite pet, a boa constrictor, with half of its body inside Margaret's car.

"Move that snake out of here!"

"Don't blame my snake! You should keep your one ton baby hippopotamus in the pond," replied Kent, turning around with his snake and walking back to his bungalow, visibly annoyed.

After that evening, Margaret never saw or called Marvin again. Marvin didn't care; he had received a letter from Jose's granddaughter. They had been good friends and classmates from elementary school through college. She had become a veterinarian. Kevin had invited her to visit the farm in South Africa. They were in need of a veterinarian; and most importantly for Marvin, of a good dear friend.

21

Dummy's Luck

CYRIL WAS A FOLLOWER. THERE WAS NO reasoning in his decisions; he just followed leaders, never thinking why or the consequences. People saw him as an easy going youth, not too smart but pleasant.

When his teachers and school counselor noticed that he wasn't college material, they convinced his unwed mother to transfer him to a vocational school. There he quickly made friends and began following Perry. Perry was a year older than him, street wise, and bossy, but with the same low IQ as Cyril. They both were assigned to landscaping maintenance classes.

After a few months the class was sent to work on the lawns of the wealthy neighboring town under the supervision of an instructor. That day they worked on the grounds of a mansion whose owner was a heavy contributor to the school activities. A neighbor walked over and introduced himself to the group. "I'm John; you are supposed to work on my lawn after you finish here. I just ordered a catering company to bring lunch for everyone."

"Thank you, sir," the instructor shook hands with John. "By the way, there is a small tree at the back of this yard that is dying; we want to cut it down, but there is nobody at home to give us the okay."

"My neighbors went on a short vacation. They asked me to watch their home; just go ahead and remove it."

The truck with the food showed up; it was a welcome break for the class and a thoughtful gesture from a stranger. John was a nice, old gentleman; when they began to work on his lawn, he sent a servant with cold drinks for the group.

Back at the school Perry approached Cyril. "Hey Dude, did you hear about the faggot neighbor that bought us lunch? He said there's no one home where we cut that tree down."

"Yeah Dude. Why did we cut their grass if there was nobody there?"

"You got a point, Dude. But I got an idea; we can go back tonight and take some things from the house. Rich people got no idea what they have; they won't miss a fucking damn thing."

Perry turned off the lights of his parent's car as he entered the mansion driveway. He broke in through the kitchen door; Cyril followed him. "See how easy it was to get in? The queer neighbor next door must be asleep."

"Man, you're so cold!" Cyril walked behind Perry, who carried a flashlight. "These people must be loaded; this house is so big."

In the living room, on the fireplace mantle, they spotted two ornate bronze urns. They opened them up. "Dude, it looks like cocaine," said Perry burying his finger into the white powder. He tasted it with the tip of his tongue. "Have you ever done coke?" he asked Cyril.

"No, Dude, but I'd like to try it," Cyril dipped his finger into the white powder from the urn he was holding, and put it in his mouth. "It has no taste, Dude…I've seen in the movies they use their noses to suck it in; maybe we have to try that."

"You're right, let's have a coke party before we look for the things we are going to take back with us."

As soon as Cyril and Perry sat on the couches, each holding an urn, the living room was suddenly flooded with bright beams of lights from police cars outside. The young thieves had just broken into a heavily secured electronic alarmed property.

Their day in court went fast. They were charged with breaking into a residence and trying to steal the urns with the cremated remains of the homeowners two German Shepherds. Cyril's mother and Perry's family never showed up in court. But John, the wealthy neighbor, did – he hired the lawyers to defend the pair of idiots. Perry had a long criminal record; he was sentenced to do time in a correctional facility. Cyril was released under John's supervision.

Cyril, as mandated by the court, moved in

with John and became John's servant. He did it reluctantly – was John a queer?

"Cyril, I'm going to have private tutors to educate you at home. Two years from now you'll be an adult, free to move out if so you desire. Do you have any problem with that?"

Sir, are you a faggot?" Cyril asked. "I don't do those things."

John exploded in a hearty laugh. "I know many highly educated people sometimes appear suspiciously gay; but to ease your mind, I'm not a homosexual. I like the ladies. I lived a happy life with my wife until she died. We didn't have children but we had each other. I missed her dearly."

Cyril discovered a new world. Away from the life of his careless, undereducated mother, his brain began to expand into new horizons. He would never be bright, but was getting smarter.

John and Cyril traveled around the world. John treated Cyril with the affection he would have given a biological son.

Cyril's mentor died long after legally adopting him. He left a generous part of his wealth to his adoptive son. John thought he was going to leave one dummy more among the many ones from wealthy families; the ones always covered in the news for their scandalous lives. Fortunately, Cyril had become a responsible, scandalous free young man.

22

B. S. Speaker

BRENDON'S NATURAL ABILITIES WERE AT odds with his life dreams. It was nothing new in his family; his mother, Rachel, saw herself being a famous ballerina since her early childhood. She treasured her photos as a kid posing in her ballerina costume. But anyone with sharp eyes could have predicted then how the lovely, smiling, angelic child in the photos would grow into a large woman, killing her dreams. When she felt down, Rachel would pull out photo albums from childhood and nostalgically contemplate what could have been.

Wilt was Brendon's father. As a boy he was a skinny kid with acne on his face and a deep melodious baritone voice. Wilt was highly admired in his high school and church chorus groups, until he had to perform as soloist. Unable to control himself, he would then break down, sounding pitchy and insecure. It was a major disappointment for him and his parents, who wanted to have him singing in their funeral parlor. Wilt took with resignation his failed singer's dream. True to family tradition, he accepted the offer to work at their funeral parlor as an embalming apprentice. He later became a funeral director. His deep soothing, baritone voice was perfect for consoling their mourning clients.

Brendon wasn't a promising performer artist like his parents; nevertheless, he did have a dream, one that he thought he could make a reality. He put in long hours at his job, but when he was alone in the embalming room, he practiced the skills needed in front of corpses – his dream was to be a motivational speaker.

Brendon's concerned coworkers – the husband and wife team of embalmers who were training him went to Wilt's office. "How can I help you?" Wilt welcomed them.

"I don't know how to put it," the wife said with strained voice, looking at her husband for help.

"Does this have anything to do with Brendon?" Wilt asked, wrinkling his eyebrows.

"Your son is acting weird," the husband jumped. "Maybe it is nothing serious but we thought you should know."

"In what sense is he acting weird?"

"I guess the job is getting to him; we caught him talking to corpses several times," the wife added.

Wilt, a serious no nonsense man, broke into a laugh. "He must be polishing his voice to take over my job. That'll be great! I've been hoping to join a barber shop quartet; but as of now, I hadn't found time to do it. I spend most of my days consoling my clients."

Unexpectedly, Brendon was promoted from embalming apprentice to assistant funeral director. Wilt patiently taught his son many techniques to address the grieving families. Brendon learned quickly, but when it came time for delivery he fell apart; his mind went blank, and the few words he struggled to put together sounded incoherent.

Wilt sent his son back to his job as an embalming apprentice. Brendon didn't mind; in his spare time he began studying how to overcome the fear of public speaking. He joined a local Toastmaster Club to learn the trade. He dressed appropriately, spoke clearly, and repeated the theme's message several times. He kept the speech funny and lively, avoided long pauses and filler words like: um, uh, eh. Brendon also learned that if he forgot what to say next, to wear a rubber band around the wrist and snap it. The technique was called "thought stopping"; it should distract him from thoughts of anxiety and fear, and would hopefully bring back his memory. If nothing worked, he would finish his presentation the best he could, forget to collect his speaker's fee, and leave with the impression of having delivered a great speech. Next day, he would sign up for hypnosis sessions to work on conquering his fears and anxieties.

Forget the local Toastmaster Club, Brendon thought after having learned the trade. I have enough corpses here for an audience. He looked at the corpse of the man with a serious face and deep, hypnotizing green eyes. The man's eyes seemed to follow Brendon as he moved around the room improvising a motivational speech about life and death. As he ended the part of the speech outlined for jokes, he looked at the man's green eyes. Convinced he caught him smiling; Brendon left the room scared, but happy to have succeeded. If he could make dead people smile, he could for sure do better with the living ones.

23

A Master's Hand

THEY WERE TWO SMALL RURAL TOWNS; the wealthy one stood at the top of the hill looking down at the blue collar town. Besides prosperity, nature had conspired to physically separate the two towns through the abrupt ravine that made it impractical to build direct roads to connect them.

The blue collar population resented the arrogance of its uphill neighbors. Their town ran along a river, which could have been an asset if it wasn't for its murky polluted waters and its banks trashed with old tires, junk cars, rotten mattresses and a variety of small waste, more visible and foul smelling during summer.

Nature also had rewarded the uphill habitants with a clear view of the green valley and its spots of tiny villages zigzagged by the river; from the distance it was an idyllic panoramic scenery. They sure had everything that was lacking downhill.

Matthew tired of his bohemian life, had moved from Philadelphia to the uphill town, looking for a peaceful atmosphere to live and locate his art studio. He was well known and respected; his paintings were in demand in galleries worldwide.

Unfortunately, his pony tail, hippie way of dress and weekend painter friends visits to him was detrimental to his acceptance in his aloof neighbor's eyes. He had bought a large Victorian home with the intention to remodel it to serve as his painting studio and residence, but finding some elusive point in the strict town's code; the City denied him the permit.

Frustrated by the refusal, he drove the back roads to the downhill town. He enjoyed the pub's meal, drinks and the outgoing company of the regulars. They were a gregarious bunch of warm happy earthy people that welcomed him with open arms. They laughed loudly when he told them about his experience in the uphill town.

"Listen Matt," one of his new pub friends said to him, "our town smells like shit in summer, but we are people with heart, a close bunch of old good buddies. You talk and look at life as we do; you should move down this way."

"Yeah, we got some old hippies in town. Your pony tail and style of clothes will blend easily with theirs," added the other man.

"Here we don't know much about painting, but we have plenty of homes that need it," said a third one with a healthy laugh.

"Screw those uphill snobs. We have only one construction code in town: here If you build or renovate, you have only to guarantee the town that the roof wouldn't collapse," the pub's owner joined the conversation.

Matthew rode around town with two of his new pals. He found beauty in the beat up houses and quickly settled for a large abandoned colonial, facing the town's square, not too far from the pub.

Mathew drew and sketched the remodeling he wanted to do in his new property. The town had a supply of skilled unemployed construction workers that quickly transformed his property into the one he had dreamed of.

"This house looks better than the properties uphill," remarked the pub owner, while he and the pub regulars followed Matthew through it. "It's so rich in light."

Matthew inaugurated his new residence with a party in it attended by his artist pals and his new town's buddies. One of his artist friends, also a painting appraiser, stood fascinated in front of one of the many paintings hanging on the walls.

"It's a copy of Michelangelo 'La Pieta'," said Matthew stopping at his side. "I bought it in an estate sale in the uphill town. I paid $55 dollars for it."

"Congratulations, you hit the lottery."

"Why?"

"It's an original unfinished Michelangelo's painting."

"You are kidding me!"

"I'm serious; I'll bet my house on it," he assured Matthew.

Matthew's surprise lasted a few seconds.

"Let's keep quiet until I confirm its authenticity," he begged his friend.

A group of Matthew's artist buddies, impressed by his renovated colonial, stayed in town looking for abandoned properties to buy. When they moved into them, it attracted more artists into town. Overnight the old ghost town got a badly needed new blood infusion. The avalanche of young artists made the town an interesting colorful place to live or visit, especially when they painted murals on their properties' outside walls.

The exhibition of Michelangelo 'La Pieta' and the just moved in artist's paintings, daily musical concerts, and plays attracted daily crowds. The public Exhibition Gallery and Concert Hall – where most events took place was a town renovated structure of a closed mill factory, financed by Matthew using the Michelangelo painting as collateral.

Pennsylvania State started the cleanup of the river pollution. The opening of restaurants and factory outlets in the remodeled-old-brick abandoned steel plants completed the town transformation. The uphill town people began to mingle with the locals and tourists, now lamenting to have caused Matthew to move from their town, taking with him the Michelangelo's painting just appraised for $20 million dollars.

24

The Naked Shrink

EVELYN, A COLLEGE GRADUATE IN COMPUTER science, was frustrated at the program she was working on. For some reason, it ran intermittently into a loop at the very end of it. She had been trying unsuccessfully to solve the problem during the morning; by midday, her head was spinning and ready to blow. That Friday she hoped to finish before lunch and then leave to enjoy the weekend. The way it was going, she might even have to work during the weekend.

Charles, the owner of the software consultant firm, was pouring sweat at his computer next to hers.

"We are at the end of the project and suddenly nothing is working," Charles said, as he took off his damp jacket. His round, chubby face was red. "We need to turn the project in today or face heavy penalties," he added in anguish, taking off his glasses to wipe the sweat from his face. "I feel like running to the bar, getting drunk, and forgetting the whole damn thing."

Evelyn, feeling as much pressure as her boss, took off her suit jacket. Charles red face lit up further, as if on fire. Evelyn's thin blouse, wet by her nervous sweat, stuck to her skin enhancing her suave, sensual cleavage. She noticed Charles' eyes glued to her bosom, enchanted by it.

Evelyn had graduated college with a major in computer science and a minor in psychology. She lacked the funds to pursue further what she had discovered after graduation to be her true vocation – a psychology major. She would rather be in touch with human beings than cold machines.

While in college, she used her hobby to analyze her boyfriends. It was easy and fun for her to read their minds and anticipate their reactions. Most of the male students attracted to her soon became her play toys. There were girls physically better looking than Evelyn, but lacked her ability to tinker with the boys' minds. Suddenly she realized psychology had provided her a powerful advantage.

Charles swayed as he stood up from the computer – his legs were weak and shaky. He was a short man with a pronounced pot belly, a bossy personality, and a huge ego. He was sweating copiously. Against his will, he called his emergency team of programmers for help, with his eyes still enchanted by Evelyn's delicate breasts. His bruised ego and raw animal instincts would prove lethal. He began feeling dizzy and steadied himself by barely hanging onto the console rack for support.

"Let's go to the cafeteria and relax," said Evelyn, as she rushed to hold him by his arm. Charles, although in pain, felt her touch, managed to look at her eyes, and smiled before collapsing. He was taken from the computer lab on a gurney to the hospital.

Teddy, Evelyn's boyfriend and the leader of the emergency programmer's squad, cleared the software problem and returned the finished project.

"From what you're telling me, Charles succumbed hard to your charms," he joked with Evelyn. They were sitting in the hotel's restaurant across the street. Teddy was a casual type of guy. He had a pony tail, a worry free attitude, and was immune to Evelyn's psychological games. He was a strange mixture of genius and playboy.

"Please, don't joke about that. The incident made me quit programming. I don't want to see a computer again. I hate them!"

"Wow, so are you going full speed with your on line therapy project?"

"Yes… Are you still working on that job with the Wall Street investment firm? Those guys sit the whole day in front of a computer screen, they are the ideal type of patients I need; wealthy and under stress. Would you promote my services to them?"

"I'm with you, baby. I 've been working with Charles for so long that I can supply you with a ton of his clients from Wall Street as prospective patients, or should I say clients?"

"Stop joking. I'm not on the move. The word 'clients' sounds like I'm a prostitute; I'm a professional psychologist attending 'patients', not clients, remember that."

That weekend Teddy set up the split video internet communications software in Evelyn's apartment laptop. He called one his pals, a young stock broker, to try the system out with him. Evelyn sat in front of the video camera in a leather chair, dressed in a professional business suit with short skirt. She wore lenses that gave her an intellectual aura, and displayed an innocent smile. She held a yellow legal pad on her lap and a pen. It became immediately obvious that Teddy's friend was fascinated by Evelyn's long, defined crossed legs. He was enjoying her beauty, but felt ashamed to make it known.

"Errol, please I want you to feel at ease with me," she told him. As your psychologist, I see you feel insecure in front of me, and probably all the young women you meet." Evelyn noticed Errol's shy smile changed into a grimace of admission. "I want you to look at me as one of many admirers of your talent, wealth and personality." His face turned into confusion; did the rest of the world take him for that type of a guy? "I want you to believe in yourself, and the magnetism you project among young women. I'm going to take off my jacket; you will look at me as my seducer, as a man in command of this moment."

"Hi, Teddy," Errol approached him at the computer.

Teddy was testing a new program in Errol's investment company. "I want to thank you for introducing me to Evelyn. She has transformed me into a ladies man. Now she has so many patients from Wall Street that it's hard to make an appointment with her."

"Yep, she is doing great, man."

"Is she your girlfriend? I mean, are you guys planning to get married?"

"Why do you ask?"

"You know, you and I have been good pals for long time. My bosses now are her patients. They allege she is stripping in front of them during their psychology session – I mean getting completely nude! It must be hard on somebody without your temperament to accept that. I really admire you for being able to deal with your fiancés' work.

Teddy's first impulse was to punch Errol out. Although he was hurt by his friend's rude, unrequested comments, he cooled off. He had taken over Charles' business, and Errol's company was an important client. Besides, although he suspected Evelyn's online therapies had turned into a kind of interactive internet porn, he hoped his suspicions were wrong. He excused himself to go out and took a long walk. When he returned, he had decided to break his engagement with Evelyn; no man in his right mind would want a mother like her for his children.

25

Gin and Tonic and the Sea

IT WAS FORECAST AS A HOT SUMMER weekend. Laurent and Kinka filled the cooler with ice, tonic, orange juice and imported beers. Inside their cruiser's cabin, the bar was stocked with a rich assortment of liquors. Life was treating the middle-aged, upper middle class couple nicely, especially now that their two daughters were happily married. They had, through successful investments, made a respectful fortune that allowed them to retire at an early age. They had complete freedom to live their lives and do things that as young parents they couldn't – the 35-foot luxury boat was a testimony to this. During summer they used to depart from the Newport Marina in Jersey City, toward the South Jersey Shore and spend days on the boat. In winter they would navigate south to Florida to continue the enjoyment of sea adventures.

As they left the pier that Saturday morning

and hit the open sea, Kinka ascended the cabin with two tall glasses of gin and tonic. They already had been drinking with their boating friends at the marina before departing, but they felt they could handle another round – one more drink now was no big deal.

"For our freedom," Laurent lifted the glass.

"For our love," Kinka raised her glass with an eye wink and a mischievous smile. After emptying the glass she took her bikini off and lay on the deck in front of him for a sunbath. She closed her eyes and seemed ready to fall asleep. Suddenly she lifted her head, "Honey, before going to our spot on the South Shore, can we circle around the Statue of Liberty?"

"What changed your mind?" he watched her putting her bikini back on.

"Remember, that was the place where you shared your caring and true feelings for me and we kissed for the first time."

"I do remember," he said yawning. He was beginning to feel the effect of all the cocktails they had had that morning.

"You don't seem too enthusiastic."

"The traffic around the Statue of Liberty is always very congested. There are some idiots that drink too much and don't observe the rules. They seem to always show up around there."

"Oh, darling, but we are careful with our drinking and know how to avoid the dangerous boaters. Would you like me to bring you another gin and tonic?" she looked at him with a sweet smile.

"Not now. Let me turn the boat toward the Statue of Liberty."

As they motored close toward the island, Kinka observed the speeding tourist cruiser and the large wake it made. "Hey! It's coming straight toward us!" she shouted at Laurent.

"I should get out of his course," he quickly replied.

"He should yield, not us," protested Kinka.

As the distance shortened, she saw the happy faces of the thrilled tour boat passengers, about 50 of them. They raised their arms celebrating every time the craft crested a huge wave. As the cruiser got closer to their boat, it made a sharp turn. "Watch out for the boat wake!" Kinka shouted to her husband while grabbing a boat cleat to cling to. She suddenly felt the huge wave violently lift their craft several feet upwards. The cruiser shook in the air, and then landed atop of an 18-foot boat with a loud crash.

Laurent, in shock, saw the panicked faces of the tourists on that side of the Island. They had just witnessed how the 35-foot craft had leveled the smaller boat with a crew of four. Only one of them had escaped by diving into the sea. He was screaming in horror for help.

Kinka ran to embrace Laurent. They stayed paralyzed at the wheel observing the harbor patrol boats approaching. The Coast Guard and a rescue tug boat arrived later to release the crushed smaller boat caught under the keel of theirs. The dead bodies of the other three passengers were found pinned in the small broken hull of the boat.

Laurent, still in shock, and after failing the

breath test, was arrested for boating under the influence of alcohol. He was sentenced to serve a year in a minimum facility prison.

Kinka and their two daughters visited Laurent regularly once a week at the prison. They did their best to try to distract him from dwelling on his guilt of accidentally killing three people. Kinka during her husband's trial and in her visits to the prison, tried to assume the responsibility for the tragedy without success. Soon, she started missing the visits to the prison. Tormented by guilt, she had begun to drink heavily. The daughters saw how their mother's excessive drinking was deteriorating her both mentally and physically. Sadly, on one of the many trips they took her to the hospital intoxicated, she passed away.

Laurent after serving his sentence, with his life shattered, decided to volunteer for a humanitarian mission overseas. No matter how hard he tried to distract his thoughts from Kinka, the smiling face of his wife sprang into his mind. After five years overseas, he flew back home. His two daughters and his grand-children welcome him. He felt in the smiling faces of his grand-daughters the spirit of his wife – that childish, mischievous smile pierce in his soul. At that moment he realized he wasn't alone any longer.

26

It Takes a Thief to Catch a Thief

"WE NEED TO PREVENT EMPLOYEE THEFT," the president of the department stores emphasized to his staff. "We are in a very competitive field; we cannot keep raising prices to cover theft losses…any suggestions?"

"I think it takes a thief to catch a thief," expressed Julius, a junior staff member. "He would have to think like someone who would steal, and then identify the most likely theft areas in our stores."

"Good reasoning Julius. Do you have anyone in mind for that job?"

"I know somebody that may be interested. He is looking for a chance to straighten his life"

Marvin fresh out of college, had been lucky to find a job as a junior accountant in an auditing company. His salary was low, but he enjoyed being trained to scan the corporate accounting books, trying to detect how employees could access their firm's cash inventories, and other vulnerable assets to steal. He was also being taught to set up tight theft deterrent controls.

Marvin shared an apartment with two friends. One night they decided to rent a car to attend a party in the city outskirts. They had a great time at the party that lasted until late hours. Before driving home they took off their jackets and laid them in the car's trunk. Back at their building they opened the trunk to get their jackets and to their surprise, they found a cat lying over them! He was overly friendly and looked at the three men with a tender innocent expression. Marvin picked up the cat with no idea of what to do with him.

"It's late; let's return the car to the garage and bring the cat with us. Tomorrow we'll figure it out what to do with him," one of them suggested.

As soon as they walked into their apartment, Marvin put the cat on the floor. The cat roamed through the three rooms and then took possession of a pillow that lay on the living room floor – he had found his bed!

Next day the three friends left the apartment in a hurry to go to their respective jobs. The cat stayed as the sole occupant of the apartment. They had left a pot with water and a plate with pieces of chicken on the kitchen floor, and also the window slightly open so the cat could go out and lie on the fire-escape and enjoy the sun and fresh air.

When one by one they returned from work, they were welcomed by the cat with a present: The cat dropped at their feet several different women' panties!

"Mine is a no-line bikini!"

"Mine is a classic French cut!"

"I don't know what style is mine, but it sure looks sexy."

After they stopped laughing, Marvin wondered, "What are we going to do with these panties? We have to return them."

"To whom? You have to be careful, women are touchy about their underwear," one of the roommates warned him as he chuckled.

"Look at the cat; he seems so innocent, and he is so friendly. Let's keep him for a while," suggested the other roommate. "What should we call him?"

They decided on "Norman". Soon after Norman's arrival the building suffered a series of burglaries. One day, as the three of them returned from work, they were arrested by the police. A woman neighbor had seen one of her panties on the fire-escape in front of their kitchen window. The police had already searched their apartment and besides the panties, they found under the bed a large quantity of the stolen jewelry.

The jury and the judge never accepted the roommates' story that Norman was the thief. Because of no previous arrests, each of them received the minimum punishment, a three year prison term. Julius, the boyfriend of Marvin's sister, volunteered to take care of Norman.

After getting his sentence reduced for good behavior and set free, Marvin gladly accepted the security job at his future brother-in-law's company.

Marvin took Norman to the different department stores hoping his cat would steal merchandise, and thus give him leads of the areas in need of better protection. To his surprise, Norman refrained from stealing; instead he began curving his tail and pointing to the thieves visiting the stores.

Once assured of Norman's honesty and accuracy, Marvin took him to roam free in the different stores. A back up security guard watching on the surveillance cameras would order the arrest of the person Norman's tail would point to. Meanwhile, at the retail store's principal office, Marvin began scanning the accounting books to catch the inside thieves. By accident, Marvin and Norman have formed a spectacular anti-burglary team.

27

A Matter of Trust

JERRY GREW UP IN A FOSTER HOME. After graduating from high school he went straight to the Army. His decision was triggered by many emotions: love for his country, lack of family life and a broken teenage romance that left him badly hurt.

The Army tough basic training swept away all Jerry's anxieties. The rigorous physical training allowed him to sleep soundly at night with no energy left to care for his soul wounds. He felt happy; the Army provided him with clothes, hot meals and comrades – it quickly felt like home.

As he was settling in with his army life, he was notified and prepared to fly to Iraq. There the reality of war hit him hard. He witnessed his buddies being blown apart by road bombs, and civilian (especially women and children) killed in crossfire – life was cheap!

When he finished his military duty, he returned to the states and tried to readjust to civilian life. He soon realized his emotional disposition was not up to the new change. He reenlisted in the Army for another tour of duty. The Army sent him back to Iraq where his mental condition continued to deteriorate further. He was discharged a few months later and sent back home for mental treatment at an Army medical hospital. The depressing hospital environment made him feel even worse, and one day he decided to run away and vanish among the homeless roaming the streets of New York City.

Camille was a middle-age advertisement executive. She lived a happy comfortable married life. She had succeeded in accomplishing an impressive career in her advertisement job. Her husband, Fred, had built a respectable middle size construction firm through years of hard work and sweat. They had only one son who had graduated from college and moved out of state to work for a large corporation. He was married, had two children, and was well established. Camille and Fred were not a materialistic couple, they just loved their jobs. They felt blessed that working in what they liked had rewarded them both with a solid financial future. They were planning to work a few years more and then take early retirement.

At lunch time Camille waited outside the lobby of her firm for a coworker. They had decided to go to a SoHo restaurant for a light lunch. While waiting, her coworker called Camille; she was expecting a client phone call and would meet her a few minutes later at the lobby entrance. Camille didn't mind; it was a sunny nice day to stand on the street. She distracted herself watching people passing by. She noticed the young homeless man breaking from the crowd and approaching her.

"I'm sorry to bother you. I haven't eaten in two days. Could you spare me with some change?"

Camille stared at the young beggar. Somehow he reminded her of her son; they could be of the same age. The young beggar looked clean in his blue jeans, denim jacket and work shoes. Only his unruly hair, wild beard and the plastic bag he held with his few belongings confirmed his misery. She guessed he was wearing the clothes given to him by some charity organization.

"Please, wait," she asked him while checking her purse. "I don't have any change."

"Thanks anyway," the young beggar turned to walk away.

"Don't go; I want to help you," she took out her debit card. "I'm going to give you my card and my code number. Withdraw $20 dollars for your food. The bank is two blocks away. I'll be waiting for you here."

The people standing near to her outside the lobby looked at her in disbelief as the young man walked away.

"He could clean out your account," one of them said to her. "I'll escort you to the bank to make sure he doesn't do it."

"Thank you, but I trust him."

"I hope you're right," said another witness. "It

may turn into a very expensive mistake."

Camille's friend came out of the building. "I'm sorry for my delay," she excused herself. "Let's go for a nice lunch."

Camille told her about her debit card.

"Are you crazy! Let's walk to the bank to get your card back." She replied. There was no need for it; as she finished her sentence the young beggar showed up card in hand to return it.

Next day Camille and Fred waited for Jerry outside the building lobby. She had told her husband about the debit card incident and insisted he meet the young beggar. "He reminded me of our son. You can hire him to work for you." She glanced at her wrist watch, "He promised me to come back today."

"I hope he does; I can always use the help of an honest man," Fred said "If he accepts my offer we can lend him our son's bedroom until he gets established," he added while noticing Jerry approaching them.

28

Kitchen Affair

TONY HAD HIS MIND IN SYNC WITH HIS priorities; a remarkable feat for a creative man whose brain was always boiling with ideas while his sense of organization worsened. In Tony's mind, his primary interest was a toss between the restaurant he owned in partnership with his wife, and his love for somebody who he had become crazy about. As number three he listed his two sons (both spoiled high school drop outs) and his ancient always whining mother Camille.

Last on the list was Diane, his wife, all brains with strong business skills. She boasted that the reason the restaurant was surviving Tony's erratic behavior was her strong leadership. She was also very judgmental, "You always run from the kitchen to welcome our clients with free cocktails when an attractive woman shows up with them. Think with your brain instead of your other thing," she would scold at him.

"You're just jealous of my social skills; it's my friendliness that brings our clients back."

"You're wrong, it's your food. You are a good chef."

She was stingy when it came to compliment him. He thought of himself as a great chef. But besides not recognizing his talents, his wife had become distrustful and cold toward him. Diane mistrusted Tony so much that she had taken over the responsibility of hiring the restaurant personnel. She knew the type of woman that would boil Tony's blood and was careful to avoid them. Her last employee hired was the pastry chef. She looked so innocent and nondescript with her librarian type of glasses, shy personality and skinny long legs. Tony liked wild women with rich curves; that motivated Diane to hire Gisele, overlooking her lack of experience. Diane even thought that Gisele could be a good company for one of her two sons, both of them as wild as their father when it came to choose girlfriends. Diane's right decision to hire Gisele was confirmed when Tony came to her complaining about the new pastry chef's skills, "This skeleton makes pastries like cement blocks. You better fire her before we get sued for breaking our clients' teeth."

"She will get better, just be patient." Diane smiled inwardly.

Tony kept quiet; Diane had caught him hitting on the former pastry chef. It was better to accept the presence of the skeleton in his kitchen than risk bringing back recent bad memories.

Tony decided to stay over when the restaurant closed to give the skinny girl training to improve her pastry skills. She took it seriously. Tony, as he watched her whipping the eggs, wondered about his taste for women. Skinny girls dominated the modeling fashion ideals. Maybe he was too old fashioned on his taste and appreciation of current women's beauty standards. Now and then, Gisele would take her ugly thick glasses off to wipe her sweaty brow from the kitchen heat, revealing her beautiful green eyes and delicate face. Tony felt his blood was beginning to boil again.

That early morning, as they had done for the last six months, Tony and Gisele drove over the George Washington Bridge on their way to the Hunts Points Terminal Market to buy the provisions for that day's menu. The euphoria of being in love, kissing, laughing and singing in the van was gone some time ago. Tony had separated from Diane to share a small apartment with his pastry chef lover. He had bought back with a bank loan Diane's half ownership of the restaurant. Unfortunately for them, after Diane left, the restaurant had fallen into hard times. Tony had missed several bank loan payments, creating pressures between him and Gisele.

When Tony and Gisele walked into the meat distributor, the owner approached him, "I'm sorry Tony, I cannot give you more credit. You haven't paid the old bills. Anything you buy now must be in cash."

Tony neither had cash nor credit cards (the

latter had been canceled by the banks). He got the same response with the vegetable and fruit distributors. Empty handed, they made the return trip to New Jersey. When they approached the George Washington Bridge, Gisele asked Tony to stop. She silently got off the van.

"Where are you going?" Tony asked.

"I have a brother in Manhattan; I'm moving in with him," she replied walking away toward the subway station.

Tony, confused, headed onto the bridge. Halfway through it, he stopped the van again.

Diane was watching the morning news at home when she saw Tony ready to leap off the bridge. A group of policemen, from a short distance, were trying to dissuade him. She ran to her car and headed to the bridge. Tony's suicide attempt had caused a monumental traffic jam extending for miles. Riding inside a patrol car, Diane approached the spot where Tony was trying to regain courage to finalize his suicide attempt.

"SOB jump now! I'm late for my job," she heard a furious motorist yell at her husband. Others were showing their rage blowing the horns nonstop.

Diane got close to Tony. "You idiot! Have you noticed the mess you are causing? Come down from there." Tony silently obeyed his wife and tried to walk close to her, hiding his shame, head down like a scared little kid.

29

Pamper Market

BRADLEY PASSED THE NEW YORK STATE BAR examination after two failed attempts. He needed a job badly to support his wife. His family had been sustaining them for the past three month, although they despised her.

Sally was demanding. Coming from a drunken mother and a blue collar stepfather, she dreamed about a wealthy comfortable life – one her parents couldn't afford to give her. She was also feeling tired of all the one night stands and wise guys she had dated from her neighborhood, interested only in enjoying her body. She needed to settle down with a husband able to provide her with the means to a prosperous life. That motivated her to pursue Bradley, the son of the owners of the most popular delicatessen in the neighborhood. He was boring, but educated enough to be successful.

Bradley was hired by a full-service law firm.

They trained him to work in family law. The first client the firm assigned him was serving time in prison. He went to visit Stuart doubting his abilities as a defense lawyer; Bradley knew he lacked the ability to sound witty and convincing, something he hoped to cure with experience.

Stuart was a middle-aged entrepreneur, involved in running a baby-selling business. Bradley‘s immediate impression of him was that of a streetwise and mean man; his visit to him, contrary to his desire, lasted too long.

Right after his prison visit, he returned home. As he walked through his apartment, he was struck by Sally’s mess. Her clothes were spread all over the place; in the kitchen there were dirty dishes waiting for him to wash. Sally’s club music, coming from the bedroom, blasted the walls of their tiny apartment.

“Did you bring food?” Sally shouted at him over the music. She was barefoot, in panties and a tight blouse, lying over their bed. As usual, she held in one hand the ashtray, and in the other, a lit cigarette. On the night table there were empty beer cans.

“What would you like to eat?” Bradley asked her as he entered the bedroom.

She lowered the music volume. “Let me see, we already tried Chinese twice, yesterday we ate pizza, what about some ribs?”

“Did you pick up the clothes from the laundry?” Bradley asked her before going for the ribs.

"You bastard; you know I'm in my second month of pregnancy. I cannot carry anything heavy."

If you're so conscious about your pregnancy, why don't you stop smoking and drinking? he thought, but opted to keep silent.

He came back with the food and the clean clothes. He set the table, and called Sally to have dinner. She had turned off the radio.

"When are they going to give you a pay raise?" she asked as she showed up in the living-dining room, still half-naked.

Bradley stared at Sally's luscious body as she sat at the table. "My salary raise will come soon. Today they assigned me to my first case. My client is in prison, I spent a good part of the day there. He is in a large-scale baby-selling business."

"Wow! That's an easy and big money making business. I know girls in our neighborhood that got pregnant and sold their babies to those guys. Take me with you the next time you visit him. I could assist you; I know their tricks."

"He wants to hire me to advise his girlfriend; she is in charge of his business until he gets free."

Sally, very insistent, accompanied Bradley to his second meeting with his client in prison. Stuart was instantly attracted by Sally's curves. After a few minutes they wound up talking like old buddies. "My other lawyer told me he offered to pay the IRS my due taxes and their fine in exchange for my freedom. They accepted it," Stuart said to Bradley, then turned to Sally. "Money talks, baby; look at this visit, it shouldn't last more than an hour and we are already here two hours. You know, I would like to retain your husband as my legal adviser and have you as a partner in my business."

Two years later, Bradley received, in the firm's conference room, a group of women that had sold their babies to Stuart.

"He placed ads in supermarket tabloids to lure us to sell our babies. We were easy prey, abandoned by our boyfriends, with no economical recourse," one of the woman explained to Bradley.

"I still keep the ad that he used to convince me to sell my baby," another woman said, then read from it: 'Pregnant, confused, undecided? We will care for you. We'll find the right loving couple to adopt your baby. We'll provide you with free medical, housing and counseling.' He didn't take a penny from his pocket to provide us any help. He had already lined up anxious, childless couples dreaming to adopt. They covered our pregnancy expenses besides paying him a fortune for finding us."

"After we gave birth, he put us on the street penniless," added a third woman.

"I'm desperately looking for the daughter that I gave up eight years ago. I was then 16. While I was in labor I got a glimpse of her before they took my baby away and put me on the street," added another woman.

On behalf of the women, Bradley's firm had authorized him to build the class action suit against Stuart. Bradley had quit two years ago – with the consent of his law firm – his legal advisory role to

Stuart. By then, Sally and her baby daughter had moved into Stuart's luxury apartment. She had confessed in her divorce papers that her daughter's father was not Bradley, but a former boyfriend she was seeing while married to Bradley. Another lawyer from the firm – to avoid Bradley's being attacked in court as having a conflict of interest in the case – was going to represent the group of women exploited by Stuart.

30

Life Through a Pawnshop

IT WAS A FAMILY BUSINESS THAT STARTED three generations ago. Their great-grandmother, Juanita, an uneducated but shrewd immigrant from Mexico, with her hard earned savings began making loans to members of her family. Soon she faced a tough dilemma: collecting the loans and the earned interest from them. Her older son had taken the loan as a gift. She needed a quick recovery plan; otherwise, she would kiss goodbye a good part of her savings – the product of long days of sweat cleaning homes of well-to-do families seven days a week.

"Hey, Mom, could you lend me some money? I'll pay you back next week," the older son asked her.

"You haven't paid me the first loan."

"My truck needs repairs. Without my truck I cannot work. I'm your son; you have to help me."

"Give me the TV from your bedroom, your watch and your wedding ring. I'll give them back to you when you pay me the two loans."

"My TV? And what will happen if I'm late in paying you back?"

"I'll sell it with your watch and wedding ring to recover my money."

Juanita, without realizing, had discovered the system used by the town's pawnshops. Encouraged by her success, she started lending to outsiders. She had the advantage over the town pawnshops: she dealt in Spanish with her Mexican neighbors, and had no need to rent a store; hers was a home business. Juanita could neither read nor write, but she knew how to count money; besides, her privileged memory covered the need of keeping an accounting ledger.

Pancho (Frank for his American friends and associates) was doing his tour of their family pawnshops. It was part of the empire created by his great-grandmother – twelve stores spread throughout Texas. Juanita, an illiterate woman, had found a business that on bad times provided small loans to the needy charging high interests on them; and in good times – when people had money – selling items left as collateral that were not redeemed. The two sides of the pawnshop complimented each other to face any type of economical swing.

During Juanita's times, pawnshops conveyed the image of thieves trading in stolen jewelry, and down-and-out people selling their treasured possessions for hard cash. Now, the family's dozen stores looked more like a bank's branches. They made loans of mostly 50 to 200 dollars for middle-class and working-class who were cut off from credit by commercial banks. Many clients faced a shortfall triggered by a medical bill or an unexpected inconvenience. As collateral for the loan they would leave jewelry, watches, music equipment, cameras and tools, among other items. The stigma attached to the people leaving their possessions in the stores was gone. Pancho, who had graduated from college with a business degree, had made the clients feel as if they were offering their possessions on eBay. The photo of Juanita hanging on the twelve pawnshop branches, with a sweet smile, seemed to approve the changes introduced by her great-grandson. Also, she seemed to smile for having created an enterprise that employed and provided a good life for all her great-grandsons.

Pancho had gone further. He had married a girl from an aristocratic, wealthy family. Their three sons attended exclusive private schools. Pancho was doing greater business. In the privacy of his luxury office – far away from the pawnshops – he received wealthy people that had fallen into economic distress. He made them larger loans, accepting mansions, land, yachts, luxury cars and expensive jewelry as collateral.

"Good morning, Jose," Pancho walked into one of the family stores on his periodical inspections. "How are you doing?" Right away he noticed the young woman crying in front of the plexiglas protected counter. She was holding a baby in her arms. Jose stood behind the counter.

"Is everything okay, Jose?" He asked his cousin, looking curiously toward the crying young woman. Her face was remarkably similar to his great-grandmother's face, in the photo hanging behind the counter.

"Mister, I want to change my medallion for 200 dollars to take my daughter to the doctor. She woke up with a high fever," she said to Pancho with desperation.

"That medallion is not worth more than five dollars," said Jose. "Why don't you take the baby to the emergency room in the hospital?"

"Immigration is at the hospital entrance waiting for people like me," she answered.

"Come with me, I'm going to take you to my doctor," Pancho reacted, guiding her to his car, for the first time breaking the main rule of his business: never feel compassion for the clients.

31

Pepe, the Great!

PEPE WAS AN ACCOUNTANT — NOT BY preference but out of necessity. His dream was always to become a famous soccer player. He had an uncle that played professional soccer and even had the honor of being called once to play in the Chilean national team; his uncle was his inspiration.

Pepe from childhood began playing soccer in the junior divisions of his uncle's club. At age 17 his dream suddenly came to a halt; only one of his teammates was called for a tryout to join the professional team – he wasn't. It became his first rude awakening into the real adult world.

"You're not doing badly," his uncle tried to shake him out of his severe disappointment. "You are studying accounting, speak English and are an accomplished social dancer. Look at me; I did play professionally; I was good – but not good enough to play in the European leagues and make decent money – and now, after my prime time has passed, I'm making my living driving a taxi."

"I don't enjoy accounting."

"I don't enjoy driving the taxi, but I have to feed my family."

His uncle was right; his life wasn't that bad. After graduating with a degree in finance, thanks to his knowledge of English, he was hired by an American bank with offices in Chile. He enjoyed a decent salary and an active social life. The bank sent him frequently to the United States for update training in their computerized accounting systems.

On one of those trips, during a company party in New York, Ruben, an executive of a Wall Street investment firm, approached him. "You are a great dancer. I would love to dance as well as you do, but I have neither the skills nor the time to do it."

The executive's wife joined them. "I bet my husband will ask you to dance with me," she laughed. "Hi, I'm Jillian."

Pepe danced with Jillian; she was a gracious middle aged lady with dancing skills better than his. "I wish I could dance with you again; you're such an accomplished dancer," he complimented her.

"I used to compete in ballroom dancing. My husband knows I would love to do it again, but it's hard to find the right partner. Would you be interested in dancing with a woman who is old enough she could be your mother?"

"I feel flattered by your offer but at the end of this week I have to return to my job in Chile."

Ruben, to please his wife, had Pepe hired in his investment firm. He felt Pepe was a decent young man whom he could trust. Pepe after finishing his day at work would meet Jillian at a Manhattan dance studio where, under the direction of a professional choreographer, they would rehearse for competitions. Pepe's failed dream to be a famous soccer player was soon forgotten. He started envisioning Jillian and he being recognized for their Latin rhythm performances, and being invited to join up with the professional dancers' exhibitions. His new dream wasn't that farfetched; they did compete and win many trophies. It helped that Ruben had secured for them the very best choreographers in town and never curtailed the expenses they originated with their outfits and travel expenses to other towns. He would join them and become a proud supporter and enthusiastic cheerleader. Undoubtedly he was their biggest fan!

Pepe's sweet new life in the states came (as it happened in Chile) to an abrupt ending; the unexpected collapse of the 2008 Wall Street's stock market sent Ruben's investment firm into bankruptcy, and Ruben and Pepe to the unemployment lines. Sadly it served to confirm to Pepe that he had been cursed by life to live as just an average man.

Before Ruben and Jillian sold their luxury flat in Manhattan to move to a more modest home in Florida, they used their good reputations to get Pepe hired as a doorman in their building. Pepe accepted the job; it reminded him of his uncle in Chile who was forced to drive a taxi after being recognized in his club and neighborhood as a celebrated soccer player.

A few weeks into his new doorman responsibilities, Pepe received an urgent call from one of the wealthy tenants. She was suffering an asthma attack. He rushed her to the hospital just in the nick of time to save her life. "Pepe is my guardian angel," the lady praised him repeatedly after returning home.

Soon the tenants began commenting among themselves about the recently hired young doorman, "He's everything you want a doorman to be; polite, friendly, not gossip-driven and very helpful."

"Don't forget he is also handsome and looks so dignified in his doorman uniform," added an old lady. "He knows how to wear it with class yet with a casual attitude."

"You're right, dear, and his walk and posture is so graceful.
Not for nothing he was Jillian's ballroom partner; they won many awards."

Pepe, already resigned to accept the limitations of his new job, was to be surprised once more in his life, this time for a good reason. He had been voted the city's "Top Doorman" by the Service Union Local. He was honored in a ceremony attended by the New York City mayor, interviewed on TV, and had photos taken of him receiving the award from the mayor in all the city newspapers.

Fame, although short lived, yet was long in arriving and had finally tapped Pepe's shoulders, breaking his curse of life disappointments. The tenants, after his award, nicknamed him "Pepe, the Great".

32

A Grouchy Man's Happyness

"IF I DIE IN NEW JERSEY I WANT TO BE buried in Florida. If my death happens in Florida, I want to be buried in New Jersey. And I want you to read and start the distribution of my new will right after my funeral."

"Why would you want that?" His perplexed lawyer asked him.

"I want to screw my family." Nestor said bitterly. "It is pay back to my wife for her years of constant threats of leaving me if I didn't keep financing the lazy lifestyle of her and our children. I came to America young, with empty pockets. I sweated blood for every penny I made, and those bums all they want is to blow away my wealth."

"I know you want to destitute your wife as well as your two children. But, by law, your wife unfortunately will be entitled to inherit most of your fortune."

"Find something in the law to screw her as much as you can. I wound up marrying a social symbol that was a flop in bed. Her mind was focusing on preserving her looks and upbeat lifestyle, not in satisfying me. I threatened her with divorce if she didn't consent to have children. Big deal! I wound up fathering two bums!"

"Nestor, you have my sympathy; you deserve better."

"William, cut the crap out! You should be thankful that with my account you put your kids through college and financed your own fancy life. But I didn't ask for sympathy as retribution."

"I'm sorry if I upset you. Now I need to give you legal advice. You should start making generous gifts to your lady friend and the son you have with her; this way it cannot be contested as part of the will. Also you should increase your donation to the church."

"Regarding my mistress and our son, I have been doing that since I met her; but besides the money, I want them included in my will."

"Why make it public?"

"I want to embarrass my wife and our children. I want final revenge! They brag about their wealth but never credit me, the guy who made it possible. Worse than that, they treat me like a peasant in my own home. My mistress and our child are always warm to me. When I first met her, she was coming out of a bitter divorce. I told her I was single, and then she got pregnant. She insisted in having the baby, even after I admitted to having lied to her about being single."

"They have every right to be included in your new will. You should get a letter from your psychologist stating that you are in full mental health. It will prevent your family from contesting the will on those grounds."

"Good thinking! When will it be ready?"

"This afternoon. I'll give you a call. "

Nestor shook hands with his lawyer and left.

From his lawyer's office he went straight to his church. His pastor already knew he was going to leave a considerable amount to the church in his will. The pastor suspected it was Nestor's way to buy a piece of real estate in heaven. He was warmly welcomed by the pastor.

"Do you think my marbles are functioning well?" Nestor asked him abruptly, going straight to the point.

The pastor paused for a second; the left wing of the church had been remodeled with Nestor's contribution. Fortunately, he had no reason to lie; Nestor was indeed a very clever man, "Of course, God has given you extraordinary mental abilities. As you mature, they seem to have sharpened further."

"I need you to write your comment in a letter addressed to my lawyer," he asked of the pastor.

Nestor went to his office and ordered his secretary to send the pastor's letter via a messenger to his lawyer. He had just saved an expensive session to the shrink.

Now alone in his office, he called his mistress. His whole demeanor softened, his authoritarian voice lowered and mellowed, “Hi Julie, do you feel ready to go to Florida for a few weeks? I’m waiting for a call from my lawyer to sign some papers in his office. Pack our clothes and I’ll pick you up in a few hours. We’ll be flying to Florida.” During years of visits to Julie and their son at the apartment he had bought for them, Nestor had filled a closet with his clothes. It came in handy when claiming business, he disappeared from his legal family to enjoy the calming and loving company of Julie and their son.

As always, Nestor and Julie made a happy couple; they felt close and comfortable with each other. They awoke early for their daily walks on the beach. He looked at least 10 years older than her, but his attitude and relaxed mode made them a great looking couple. His mean demeanor had totally vanished; the thought of death gone; the impulse to accumulate wealth forgotten. They walked like young honeymooners holding hands, free of worries. They had made friends with other vacationing couples that joined the usual early morning walk on the beach.

Nestor and Julie in the middle of their vacation took a cruise to the Caribbean Islands. Their son came right from college and joined them. Nestor spent long hours with his out-of-wedlock son. He was a bright kid that had fully bonded with him through the years.

At the cruise’s last dinner, Nestor took a jewelry box from inside his jacket. “It’s for you.” He passed Julie a ring.

Julie received it surprised and thrilled, “You

must have spent a fortune on it."

"With that ring I'm proposing to you. I sent a text message to my lawyer to file for my divorce; I want to marry you."

33

Shared Pain

"OH, NO! THEY BURGLARIZED OUR HOME again!" Rita in tears stepped over strewn clothes, turned over drawers, opened purses and documents spread all over the floor. She called Paul at his job. He rushed back home to calm his wife and assess the damage. Paul, reacting to the emotional and material harm, made a quick decision, "We're moving!"

The couple and Jay, their ten year old son, were a religious family. They felt comfortable and happy in their apartment – in what it until then was a safe building, two blocks away from their church. Besides religion, the church provided them with most of their friends and social activities. Jay was attending a private school in the Upper East Side. A school bus picked him up every morning for the short ride to his classes. It was painful for Paul's family to leave behind their church and circle of friends; and having to miss Harlem's second renaissance: the renovation of old buildings, the opening of new retail and office space, and the return of black middle class families to their roots. But they were too traumatized by the two burglaries to stay.

They found a real estate agent that wasn't afraid to show them homes in an all-white Long Island neighborhood, and soon they were closing on a property. They moved to the new place. Rita worried whether they would be accepted in their new vicinity.

"We socialize with our white coworkers and visit their homes. They had come to Harlem to visit ours. Why would we have problems moving here?" Paul tried to calm Rita. "It's not color but education that counts now."

After they moved, they noticed different reactions. Some neighbors were cautiously friendly; others, openly hostile.

Bruno was born, grew up and married a girl from his Long Island town. Their town was a bastion preserving the culture of their ancestors. Even after his divorce, he stayed with his son in the neighborhood. His neighbors when they saw the black family moving in on their block complained bitterly, "These blacks are devaluating my property," one of them was shouting. Bruno's son, Vincent, was among the group listening; he was seventeen.

"Wait until they began throwing parties and you will see more blacks coming to our block," another neighbor added. "It takes only one rotten real estate agent to screw the neighborhood."

"These people act like animals, cursing loudly, disrespecting women and pissing on the streets," said another one.

Vincent left the upset group of neighbors to go to Bruno's auto body shop. Father and son had been working together since Vincent graduated from vocational school.

"Hey, Dad, what do you think about the blacks moving to our block?" shot Vincent as soon as he stepped into the shop.

Bruno took a few seconds to answer, "Listen, I know how the neighbors feel, but those blacks seem like quiet people."

"But what about if more blacks begin buying homes here?" insisted Vincent, trying to dissipate his disappointment with his father's opinion.

"Let's just worry about our shop," Bruno cut the conversation. "Now that you are working with me, we'll need more clients."

Jay made friends with Lisa, a classmate from the new white kid's school. Lisa, as Jay, came from a religious family. She was the only kid in the school to open up to Jay. Lisa parents' didn't object to Jay being her friend, just so it didn't go further than that – just friends. Unfortunately, soon an ugly rumor started spreading through the neighborhood – Jay had raped Lisa!

That evening, Paul's family, ignorant of the callous prank rumor, sat at the table and prayed before dinner. Shouts from the street interrupted their prayer; they heard the racial slurs followed by a stone that broke the dining room window.

"You and Jay go to our bedroom and call the police," Paul ordered his wife. He rushed for the gun he had bought after the first burglary in their Harlem home. Paul, holding the gun, opened the door, frightened by stories he had heard about Southern lynch mobs.

Rita and Jay heard the shot and people running away, then the police sirens. A police officer entered their bedroom, "Your husband has killed a young man. He is being arrested." He addressed Rita.

Rita and Jay ran to the street door. Vincent's body was lying on the entrance walkway, his face covered by blood. On the street, Paul, handcuffed, was being led in a patrol car.

Paul was accused of shooting Vincent at point blank range. He testified to have been afraid of confronting a lynch mob. Also that while trying to scare the angry mob away, his gun accidentally discharged.

After drawn-out jury deliberations, he was convicted of manslaughter and sentenced to three years in prison.

During the trial Bruno had stayed silent, immersed in the pain of having lost his only son. Since his son's funeral, he had visited his grave every day. He was convinced that his son, as well the convicted black man, had been the victims of a false, vicious prank. The real guilty person of taking his son away was the author of the prank, and he was hidden in the anonymity, like all cowards are.

34

My War's Buddy

THEY WALKED TOWARD THE PARK'S DOG run. It was a large patch of grass, fenced and surrounded by tall trees. It functioned as a place to socialize for the dog owners, and a nice, safe run for dogs to exercise. They would go through two security doors – it was a precaution to keep the dogs from sneaking out of the run. When a newcomer would open the outside door, the other door would stay closed and *vice versa*. Once crossing the second door, the dogs would be unleashed and left free to run and sniff other dogs. It was amazing to see such a large pack of different breeds and sizes playing around without picking a fight. Not to say that on rare occasions, when a dog would try to bite another one, the owner would yell, stop! If the dog didn't obey, both would be kicked out of the run.

Rudy crossed the doors with Storm. They had flown the day before from Afghanistan. When Rudy unleashed Storm he stood still, next to him, scared to move; the feeling of stepping on soft grass was new to him. The war had made the dog cautious, especially when being in unfamiliar surroundings. The landscaping of the park was so different from that in Afghanistan. There, Storm had been trained by the Army to detect road mines. Rather than run, he was taught to walk cautiously, and carefully sniffing out the explosives found in his way. He had become an expert climbing the arid rocky hills, ahead of his squad to clear the path for them.

After serving two tours in Afghanistan, Rudy was also struck by the landscaping; it was his reencounter with the green cheerful vegetation where he had grown up. He admired the tall trees, the mossy grass, and the view of the geese circling on the park's lake. There was a serene tranquility – drastically contrasting with the tense Afghanistan atmosphere.

Storm's 'stand-guard' posture fell apart when Lisa, a 100 pound of joy, came from behind to smell him. Storm reacted like a compressed spring suddenly released, jumping high while turning in the air to face the enemy. He immediately conceded to be half the weight of the Rhodesian ridgeback he was touching noses with. He growled ready to defend himself as a proud US soldier, only to be confused by Diane's passionate response. The Rhodesian ridgeback gave Storm a heavy dose of doggy drool. The stray Afghanistan dog, a breed of many mixtures, felt as he had landed in Cupid's heaven.

After salivating Storm's face at her will, the cute slobbering Rhodesian girl circled around, enticing him to chase her.

"Diane is a lover, she likes to kiss," her owner approached Rudy laughing. He turned to look at her. She had beautiful blue eyes and a friendly smile, which made her overweight figure less conspicuous. "Looks like they are enjoying playing together... Your dog has a limp," she noticed.

Storm, getting out of his initial surprise, had thrown his army- taught caution to the wind, and began chasing Diane around the large run.

"We both got it," replied Rudy, smiling back at her.

"Please, stop me if I'm being nosy, was it a car accident?"

"No ma'am, it happened in Afghanistan, I was a sergeant stationed there, and Storm was my dog…but it's a long story. I don't want to bore you with it."

"If it doesn't hurt you, I would like to hear it. I feel is unfair that our troops over there risk their lives every day, while we have it sweet over here."

"Thank ma'am for your sympathy. I'll make it brief. We were in an isolated Afghanistan outpost in Korengal Valley. It was around 9:00 o'clock at night; we were watching a movie inside the barrack. Storm and two other army dogs abruptly got up from the floor and ran outside the barrack. A few soldiers and I ran behind them carrying our weapons. An explosion knocked us to the ground. I was bleeding from my leg. Storm turned back and jump covering my body just in time when we heard a second explosion. When the chaos settled down, I noticed Storm was bleeding as badly as I. He had taken most of the shrapnel to save my life. The other two dogs had immobilized on the ground a Taliban man loaded with grenades; by doing that they had saved many soldiers' lives. We were lucky the helicopters landed soon after, and flew all the wounded to the hospital unit. Storm was treated in the hospital with the same care we had. When we recovered, the Army allowed me to bring Storm to the states."

The dogs finished exhausted after playing their games; it was time to go home. Jessica put the leash on Diane, Rudy on Storm.

"It was so nice to meet you," Jessica turned to Rudy.

"Same here, ma'am."

"Did you park nearby?"

"We walked to the park. I have to find a job, look for a place to live and then buy a car."

"Where are you staying now?"

"At my sister's family, but one of my nephews is allergic to dogs. A Veteran Financial Support Network promised me help. I'm waiting from them to look for a room."

"Unbelievable! After risking your life for your country, you have to beg to a private organization for help. Where is the government?" Get in my SUV. My parents will tell me I'm nuts, but I'm going to take both of you to my apartment to stay with Diane and me."

35

Why Us?

BETSY GRAZED PEACEFULLY IN THE FAMILY farm where she was born. She was just one more head in the herd enjoying the rich grass of Upstate New York.

It was a beautiful autumn day. The fallen golden leaves decorated the farm road with ever changing patterns; it contrasted with the vivid-lush green pastures where the herd grazed. Sadly for the cattle, the farm advertised them as grass-fed beef, claiming their meat to be lower in calories and fat, higher on Omega-3 fatty acids, quicker to cook, and with no added hormones or antibiotics – ideal for New York City gourmet restaurants or for exporting.

Betsy was resigned to her destiny. The two calves born out of her first pregnancy, as they grew up, were separated from her and taken to the threatening barn – the farm's slaughter house across the fence. One calf had escaped from the barn and fell on her knees near the fence. Bleeding from the brain, the calf looked at Betsy with glassy eyes before collapsing dead. Betsy would never forget that moment; she would have welcomed being taken to the barn in their place to save her two calves' predestined fate. Unfortunately, Betsy had again received artificial insemination and was feeling the first symptoms of her new pregnancy.

Collins and his newlywed wife, Sally, jumped in their SUV and headed toward his uncle Peter' farm three hours away in Upstate New York. As they left New York City behind, they enjoyed the rolling green fields of the farms and the feeling of space and freedom.

"I love the peaceful environment of the countryside," Sally opened the SUV's window and inhaled deeply the chilly clear autumn air. After a long pause, she looked at Collins with a smile. "I have news for you."

"What's that?"

"I'm pregnant."

Collins stopped on the shoulder of the road to embrace and kiss her.

Collins' uncle Peter was waiting for them at their family farm in Montgomery. He warmly welcomed his nephew and young wife. After they settled down he invited them for a walk. When they reached the grazing land, Sally said to Peter, "As a city girl, I always find it fascinating to watch the cattle; they look so peaceful and content."

"We try to provide them with the best possible environment."

"Look at her," Sally pointed at Betsy. "What a

beautiful cow! Her black and white color and melancholy eyes make her so adorable."

"That's Betsy, my favorite pet on the farm," Peter looked at her with pride. "Because of the nature of our business, we are not supposed to bond with the animals, but somehow I couldn't resist Betsy's charm."

Betsy came to the fence and stopped right in front of Sally. "She is pregnant again," Peter explained to Sally.

"Wow! What a coincidence, I'm pregnant too." Sally kissed Betsy's forehead. Collins captured the moment clicking his phone's camera.

"Nature is strange," said Peter. "Women and cows have a nine month pregnancy. The cows usually have two calves. I hope in your first pregnancy you aren't expecting twins, it would be too much work." Sally conspicuously smiled to Peter.

After petting Betsy for a while, they returned to the farm house where the maid had dinner waiting for them. They sat at the table. Peter addressed his nephew, "Collins, as you know, I'm alone on the farm since your parents passed away and later my wife. I'm feeling my age, ready to retire. I'm in the process of selling the farm. You will receive my brother's share of the business, unless you decide to take over our business."

"Uncle Peter thanks for the offer, but we have already settled in the city. I agree with your decision to sell it."

"What will happen to Betsy," reacted Sally.

"Sally, this is a beef producing farm. We try to give the cattle a humane environment until its time for them to be sacrificed," Peter responded to her with the softest explanation he could think of.

"Don't worry about Betsy. When Uncle Peter sells, with my share of it, we'll put Betsy and her calves in an animal sanctuary,"

Collins promised Sally, noticing how she had discretely moved away the sliced beef plate that the maid had just served her.

Eight months later Sally gave birth to twins. Collins remembering his Uncle Peter's remark about twins, called to give him the news. Their uncle's maid answered his call, "Your uncle passed away a month ago, I'm packing his belongings for donation. These are my last days on the job. His lawyer did turn the farm's keys over to the corporation that bought your farm and the adjacent ones. The lawyer said he was going to notify you shortly."

Collins, at the insistence of Sally, traveled to Montgomery. Sally desperately wanted to know Betsy's fate. Collins went straight to the lawyer's office that was in charge of his uncle will.

"Your uncle before dying asked me not to notify you of his death. He instructed me to do it after your wife gave birth," the attorney explained to Collins. "He also left a good bye note for your wife and all the legal papers from the transfer of Betsy and her two baby calves to the Animal Sanctuary Farm. They were the lucky ones to survive the slaughter. The corporation that bought the farm will raise a different breed of livestock."

36

Mismatched Emotions

THE UPPER-MIDDLE-CLASS NEIGHBORHOOD, with white picket fences and well-kept lawns, was quiet until Lucille opened the front door to let Pocho and Lula go out for fresh air and to relieve themselves under the shade of the cypress tree. The peaceful serenity of the block every day would be shattered when after visiting the cypress, Pocho and Lula would park their diminutive bodies on the center of the lawn and start serenading the neighborhood.

Pocho, a Chihuahua-Papillon combo with short caramel and white hair, big black interrogative eyes, and a tough attitude (kind of macho-man) was the tenor. Lula, a poodle-shih-tzu mix, with white thick hair a cute look and a sweet disposition, was the soprano. The two lovebirds – both rescued from a shelter – had been together since puppyhood. They had grown up – not much – under the care of Perry,

Lucille (his wife) and Camille, their daughter – a warm loving family that had pampered and spoiled them beyond imagination.

Camille had been taking private piano and singing lessons at home since she could talk. It was her dream to become an opera singer. She had been coached by several instructors. They all didn't last long, frustrated by Pocho and Lula, who would sneak in the middle of a lesson to start howling along Camille's 'Bel Canto'. Camille didn't mind, she was happy to perform accompanied by her spoiled pets. Fortunately, in town there were enough unemployed opera singers willing to provide continuous voice coaching.

That sunny midday, after visiting the cypress tree, Pocho and Lula occupied their imaginary stage at the center of the lawn, and belted their usual opening: "O Sole Mio". Lucille, from the kitchen, after listening them howling, concentrated on preparing the evening dinner. Perry at that moment was at his job, and Camille at school. Lucille had the radio on. As she switched stations to hear the midday news, she missed the howling of her pets. She walked outside expecting to see them wandering around their fenced yard. She searched the front and back yards. Then, fearing the worst, she went to the street. She walked around the block several times shouting their names with no success; Pocho and Lula had vanished.

At the police station, the sergeant called Sal, his rookie officer. "I have a job for you," he told him. "Two small dogs disappeared from their fenced property."

"Sergeant, do you mean the singing dogs?

"How do you know?"

"I know the family that owns them. Their daughter, Camille, is a classmate of my younger brother. They have posted flyers with the dogs' photos all around town, offering a nice reward for their return."

"Listen, the veteran cops don't like to be bothered looking for missing or stolen pets. Now is your opportunity to shine."

"I'll find them," the rookie cop assured the sergeant.

Sal, dressed in plainclothes, went to visit heart-broken Lucille. They walked the property. "The fence is in good shape and there are no digging marks around it. Somebody had to have jumped the fence to grab your pets."

"I don't think so; strangers scare my pets. They would run away from them."

"Your pets could have been enticed with food. But the possibility of a stranger jumping the fence waiting to attract them with food makes no sense. Who are your neighbors?

"At my right lives an old couple who always complains about the dogs hanging outside. But they're too old to jump the fence. At the other side lives a middle aged doctor. He's new on the block and keeps to himself. I don't even know his name."

Before leaving, Sal walked to the new neighbor's house. He rang the bell; nobody answered it. He opened his mailbox, and from a letter inside it, copied his name.

"Hey, kid, did you find the singing dogs?" at the precinct, a senior cop walked by Sal's desk.

"Not yet. If you hear them singing on the street, let me know."

"Don't be a wise ass, kid," the officer kept going.

Sal obtained through the motor vehicle agency the new neighbor's car insurance; company which provided him with the man's work place address. Sal drove there and introduced himself at the front desk. "I'm a police officer. Someone we arrested for burglary claimed he had tried to break into your lab facility. I need to do a quick inspection of the building to fill out my report." The building maintenance supervisor came to meet him. He checked Sal's police badge and then assigned one of his crew to walk him around.

Sal asked to be taken to the Lab where they kept the rats, rabbits, cats and dogs used in their experiments. He had searched on the internet the anguish and pain suffered by the animals at this lab while waiting for the next procedure to be performed on them. To test cosmetics and foods effects, the lab forced the animals to inhale toxic fumes and eat pesticides. Later they would cut their intestines apart while they were still alive, to study their reactions.

In an upper cage, Sal found Pocho and Lula, waiting their turn to be used for experimentation. Under the protest of the lab guide, he took them out of the cage. Holding their quivering bodies, he walked to the parking lot. As he drove away with the singing dogs, he radioed his sergeant to send a patrol car to the Lab to arrest the neighbor who snatched the dogs.

It took the singing dogs a few months to shake off their trauma and start singing again. By then, the lab, thanks to the protest of animal rights organizations, had been closed.

37

After Labor Pain

KATE WAS FEELING LABOR PAINS. TOM rushed her to the hospital. He was sweating every time he had to stop his car at a traffic light, as Kate's screaming became louder. At the hospital emergency entrance they rushed her to the maternity wing on a gurney.

After filling out the hospital forms, Tom rushed to the maternity floor trying to mentally recall the Bradley method of natural childbirth. Kate and he had attended together the classes of breathing and relaxation; he had become a husband-coach to assist her during her labor. To his surprise, he found Kate lying in bed, half asleep, and a nurse, next to her bed, holding their just born daughter. The nurse passed Karina to him. He was scared to hold his seven pounds of joy – she looked so tiny and fragile!

When the nurse left to take Karina back to her

crib in the nursery, Tom started calling Kate's family and his to share the good news. During the day, Kate's night table began to fill with flowers and good wish cards from their families and friends.

Kate woke up at midday and asked for her daughter. The nurse brought back Karina to be breastfed for the first time. That happy moment stayed vividly with Tom, and lately accompanied him when the nurse advised him to go home to rest.

Next day, just fresh from a heavy sleep, Tom rushed to the hospital, anxious to see his wife and Karina again. He stopped briefly in front of the large window of the maternity nursery. Karina's crib was empty; probably Kate was breastfeeding her. As he reached Kate's room, to his surprise, two police officers and a doctor stopped him.

"What's going on?" he reacted surprised.

The doctor explained to him, "Someone in the ward mistook your daughter for another baby…"

"What?"

"We're now checking the surveillance cameras; we'll find out how it happened." A nurse approached the doctor with a glass. "Please, drink it," the doctor asked Tom, passing him the glass. "It's a sedative to calm you down."

After following several leads with no results, Karina's disappearance became a cold case. Tom and Kate were emotionally destroyed. Tom, tortured by the memories brought back by his surroundings, moved away, out of the state. Kate decided to stay, hoping to be there when her daughter would miraculously reappear.

Constance grew up as a confused child. Her mother, Verna, was always high on drugs and alcohol, running around with different men that supported and shared her addictions. She would disappear for days, leaving Constance at the mercy of her neighbor for food and protection. Verna at that time was receiving public child support and family assistance.

Constance's school served as an escape from her miserable lonely existence at home. Thanks to the school and the good heart of her neighbor she managed to keep her sanity. Her dysfunctional life went unnoticed by her teachers and classmates – Constance was always dressed neatly with hand me downs from her neighbor's two daughters. At school they considered Constance a normal sweet girl, who enjoyed all her class activities. She was shy and extremely bright, loving to spend her after school hours in the school's computer lab until it closed for the day.

Verna in her few lucid moments, was tortured by the memories of the morning she went to the hospital to visit one of her boyfriends who was suffering from a severe drug overdose. Verna was familiar with the hospital. She had, as visitor, been there before. The reception desk was busy attending other visitors; she sneaked in without bothering to register. She got off the elevator on the last floor and walked to her friend's room. His bed was empty. Maybe he died or was discharged; either way, it didn't make much difference to her. Life was tough in her circle of friends. She had, not long ago, suffered her third miscarriage. The doctor had told her as a consequence of it she had become sterile. That killed her hope of having a child that would help her to straighten out her life. She felt the impulse to wander around the maternity wing. She took a peek in at the large nursery window. The nurses were busy taking the babies to their mothers to be breastfed. She kept walking and found herself inside a double patient room. One bed was empty and on the other a woman and her baby were sleeping. Without hesitation, she emptied a bag with clothes that she saw over a chair, put some blankets and laid the baby inside it.

Constance recently had been questioning Verna about her father. Verna had been very evasive. "He was a bad man that deserted you and me. It's not worth it to talk about that SOB."

"Did I take after him, because physically you and I have nothing in common? … Do you have a photo of him?"

Constance noticed that besides her mother's irritation, Verna got visibly nervous when she inquired about her father. Constance suspecting the worst began searching in the school lab computer for missing babies 16 years ago (her actual age). From the site of the "National Center for Missing and Exploited Children" she found Kate and Tom's baby file, with an "age projection image" of how the baby would look 16 years after her disappearance – it looked like a Constance mirror image!

The police flew Constance to her biological birth mother, Kate. A previous DNA test had confirmed she was Karina, the baby snatched at the hospital.

Tom, accompanied by his new wife, joined Kate to welcome the daughter he dreamed to find one day. Verna, by then, had been arrested and faced life in prison.

38

Anything for Georgia

CINDY RECEIVED A SURPRISE LETTER FROM someone who claimed she was her aunt from her father's side. She knew nothing about her father; her mother Karen never mentioned him. Maybe I was adopted or born out-of-wedlock, she wondered. Why had her mother kept such secret from her?

Karen had dedicated her life to raising Cindy. Cindy remembered her mother had a few suitors interested in marrying her, but nothing ever materialized – they just suddenly disappeared.

Another mystery in Cindy's life was how her mother could afford the rather comfortable living they shared, since she had never held a job. She also had managed to send Cindy to an exclusive college without worrying about its high cost. Her mother died shortly after she graduated from college with a degree as Marine Biologist. She began working as a consultant for the Wildlife Conservation Society's at the Coney Island aquarium.

After her mother's death, she lived alone for a while before marrying. Her brief marriage was more out of loneliness than love; a divorce occurred the following year.

Now single again, she had received the surprise letter from the woman claiming to be her aunt. Why had her mother never mentioned her either? Out of curiosity, she took a mini vacation and flew to California to visit her unknown aunt.

Bunny was waiting for Cindy at the airport. She rushed to embrace a surprised Cindy. How did this adorable old lady identify her? Cindy, cautious by nature, couldn't resist the genuine warm welcome. She followed Bunny to be surprised again seeing her aunt's personal uniformed chauffer waiting for them. He carried Cindy's luggage. Was "aunt" Bunny that well off?

"Oh dear, finally we met!" Bunny slowly walked toward the airport exit holding Cindy's hand and looking at her with a sweet smile. "I was able to recognize you thanks to the last photo your mother sent me. My brother would have been so happy to share this moment with us, you look so much like him."

"You will have to update me about my father; I don't know anything about him."

"My brother was a lovely man full of fun; but, oh dear, he loved women too much and too often. It caught up with him when the doctor discovered he had been infected with a fatal disease. He passed the disease to your mother, although she managed to live longer. I guess that's why she never remarried. I made it my duty to financially help your mother. She accepted my help but denied me the right to visit you. I don't blame her after the pain my irresponsible brother caused her."

Bunny had inherited a large fortune. She lived in a spacious mansion. Cindy enjoyed some of the most beautiful and fulfilling days of her life there looking at all the photo albums of her father and his side of the family until she was interrupted by a call from the Coney Island Aquarium, "We need you to fly to Alaska to pick up a three-month-old sea otter."

When Bunny learned about it she was enthusiastic. "I want to accompany you; it will help us to get better acquainted. Besides, I love otters. My husband bought me a beach house in Morro Bay, California, close to Morro Rock where there is a kelp bed near the rocks that seems to be a favorite place for the otters to take a nap. He and I enjoyed hours contemplating them; they are beautiful creatures. Since we didn't have children, we adopted them as ours."

They flew to Alaska in a private plane hired by Bunny. Once there, they rushed to meet the twelve pound baby otter – it was an adorable shiny female pup with huge hazel eyes that looked at the two women curiously.

Bunny captivated by the tiny creature ran her fingers through her rich fur, "Hi dear Georgia, you're such a beautiful girl."

Cindy couldn't stop her aunt's insistent desire to take Georgia – as she had baptized the pup – to her Morro Bay beach home. They flew back to

California in the private plane with Georgia sandwiched between them and covered with wet towels. Bunny assumed a surrogate mom role and bottle-fed the pup. After that, she groomed and cuddled her until Georgia fell asleep. While Bunny and Georgia slept, Cindy made a call to the Coney Island Aquarium. "I picked up the baby otter. She seems a little stressed; I'm going to spend a few days in my aunt's beach house with the otter to have her relax and get used to me, then I'll proceed to New York with her."

"Oh dear, I don't think I would let you take my precious daughter to New York," Bunny awoke.

Bunny's beach house had a fenced back yard with a pool. Georgia dived in it with delight; she swam with the grace of her breed and played tirelessly with Cindy and Bunny.

Next day Georgia was taken to the beach. She stepped timidly into the water to wet her paws. Cindy stayed close to her. Soon she began diving in the shallow waves and submerging to the bottom.

"Hey, look at the otters over there by the rocks," Bunny suddenly signaled to Cindy. There were about a dozen of them curiously observing Georgia's pirouettes in the nearby cove.

A week later, Cindy and Bunny with a new little bundled up pub otter boarded the plane to New York. One of Cindy's colleagues at Morro Bay Wildlife had gotten Cindy a new replacement pup to take to the Coney Island Aquarium. Little Georgia had been adopted by a female otter and had happily swam away with her.

39

Three Angels' Luck

KYLE HAD ATTENDED AND GRADUATED from a vocational school. It was quite an accomplishment for a fatherless ghetto kid. The social worker, who sent him to the vocational school, helped him to apply and get a job in the New York Metropolitan Transportation Authority – she became the first angel in his life.

His job was track maintenance in the subways' tunnels. He didn't mind working underground. He was living a dream; getting paid well and enjoying good benefits while being protected by a strong union.

His mother (she had never married) and two step-sisters from different fathers, moved with him to a safer blue-collar neighborhood. He felt proud of being the man of the house.

Unfortunately, happiness never lasted in his dysfunctional family.

A few days after moving, his two step-sisters insisted on bringing their boyfriends to live with them. He refused to do it; they threatened him with going back to the ghetto. Kyle was surprised when his mother joined them, leaving him alone in the new apartment. It was a bitter pill. He had failed to break his family's vicious circle; the women having children out of wedlock to collect welfare checks for child support.

Kyle met his future wife at his new neighborhood's church. Emily came from a closely knit family. Kyle surprised himself dreaming in the subway tunnels about a future family for Emily and himself.

Kyle's wedding was attended by a large group of coworkers. The bridegroom's pleasant personality and his willingness to help others had made him many friends. His mother and two step-sisters refused to attend the wedding in spite of Kyle continuing to help them. They feared his new responsibilities would stop aiding them.

Kyle and Emily dreamed about having children, but nature chose otherwise. Meantime Emily had made her duty to keep in touch with Kyle's family, who were cold toward him but receptive to her.

"I have bad news," Emily warned Kyle after visiting them. "Your mother is very sick."

"Are my sisters taking care of her?"

"Your younger sister moved out of their home with her boyfriend. Your mother doesn't know where she is. Your older sister and her boyfriend are both serving a life sentence for trafficking in drugs."

"Is my mom alone?"

"Sick as she is, she was taking care of your older sister's baby. He was born days before she was arrested. I brought them with me; they are resting in our guest bedroom."

Kyle learned his mother was suffering from advanced sickle cell disease. Emily took her to the hospital for treatment and also began the legal process to adopt Kyle's little niece.

Emily was compelled to take a family leave of absence from her job to care for them. Since Kyle's mother's Medicaid insurance was insufficient to fully cover her treatment, the new expenses began to pile up and take a toll on the couple's budget.

On his way back from work Kyle stopped at his neighborhood convenience store and bought a lottery ticket. So far he had had two angels in his life, the social worker and Emily. Let's hope this lottery ticket will become my third angel, he dreamed as he walked to his home.

As soon as he entered his home, he perceived the warm family atmosphere that Emily had created. His mother seemed more at peace with herself, and the baby talk and playful gestures made his wife and him feel content and complete.

Next day, while on the train to work he opened his newspaper and checked his lottery ticket. He became feverish; his third angel had touched him. He had the winning ticket! In doubt of his good luck, before reporting to work he stopped at a store and asked the clerk to check his number. "It's a loser," the clerk said to him after scanning it.

"I checked it in the paper. I got the winning number," Kyle insisted. "I just wanted you to confirm it."

"You must have checked it wrong," the clerk stood firm.

"Give me back my ticket."

"I threw it in the losers' waste basket." He leaned down and picked up a ticket. "Here it is."

"This is not my ticket!"

After a long dragged out argument with the clerk and notifying the police to the scam, Kyle heartbroken and confused returned to the store in his neighborhood where he had bought the ticket.

"You're one of my best clients," the store owner replied after learning about the dishonest incident. "I'm going to help you." He then picked up the phone and notified the lottery officials about the scam. When the State Police went to the sticky-fingered clerk's store, he had miraculously found the winning ticket. Kyle looking to heaven added up one more angel in his new happy life; the owner of his neighborhood convenient store.

40

Oh, No, It's My Baby!

GREGORY AND MARTHA DROVE ANXIOUSLY to the body shop – their precious baby was ready!

Gregory was a construction supervisor and Martha a receptionist in the town hospital. The couple's combined income – especially since the construction industry was booming – allowed them enjoy the good times, fatten their savings, and pamper themselves with classic cars. Their car hobby filled their social life. During the weekends they participated in local city exhibits and on Sundays attended quite a few benefit car shows. Also they were active members involved in the social events of the classic car owners' club. They bought cars in need of repairs or restoration through the internet and restored them in their shop. Only for major or specialized repairs were the vehicles taken to outside shops. They kept the cars and even enjoyed showing and exposing them to potential buyers. They didn't hesitate to sell them when they received good offers, making their fun hobby also a very profitable business.

Gregory had built a four car garage on his property. Two spaces were for collector cars; the third one for Martha's compact car that she used daily, and the fourth space was their repair shop.

As they entered the body shop lot, they looked fascinated at their baby, a 1957 Chevrolet sedan that they had bought for just $5,000 dollars. They had replaced the car's motor, transmission, ripped black leather seats and the racing tires, all with original parts. The body shop also had replaced the car's rusted out panels and floor pans and given the car a bright coat of fire red paint. In all, the restoration of the car had amounted to $15,000 dollars, not including the hours the couple had worked on it themselves.

"It will be emotionally hard to sell this beautiful baby," Gregory said with his eyes glued on the pristine Chevy. "I'm in love with her."

"We could easily turn this beauty over for $35,000 dollars," replied Martha, also charmed by the car's look, but more pragmatic; she was the business brain.

Raul, the owner of the body shop, timed the arrival of the couple well. He had parked their shiny Chevrolet in the center of his lot and was hand detailing and touching up its new finish, conscious of the arrival of its owners. *Estos gringos son locos por los carros,* (These gringos are crazy for their cars), thought Raul. But it's good for me; they bring me a lot of work. I need them to keep coming back.

'Hi, Raul," Gregory drove up slowly to the Chevy. "The car looks impressive."

"Thank you. You could easily sell it for $50,000 dollars," Raul exaggerated.

Gino was a frustrated young man. He had training in performing and singing, and his eyes set on Broadway productions. He had been in a few off-off-Broadway plays in minor roles, but even those presentations had dried up. He felt cheated by his luck; after all he had a college degree but felt stuck working part-time as a waiter and living in a small smelly rented room hoping for the elusive break leading to fame. On top of his misfortune, his girlfriend had just broken up with him – she had realized he was a loser!

Gino used to rent a room in the West Side of Midtown and knew the security in that building was lax. He sneaked in and rode the elevator to the last floor, then walked the stairs to the roof. Some residents of the building later told the police that they had seen a body dropping past their windows.

Gregory and Martha, thrilled by the interest their classic 57 Chevy had received at shows in New Jersey, had decided to enter their baby in a large classic car exhibition in New York, expecting good offers for it.

Martha had taken a day off from her hospital job and rode with Gregory to New York. Gregory parked the Chevy on the street, right across from the construction site where he was working. Martha took a stroll to the nearby department stores to kill time.

At midday they would have to ride their baby to the exhibition center.

"Oh, shit!" yelled several of Gregory's crew from the steel I-beam structure they were working on – they had witnessed Gino's body landing flat on their boss' slick car.

Martha had turned the corner carrying two bulging shopping bags, fully enjoying her day in the city. She heard the strange noise and began to run to her car. Her baby's roof had caved in! Gino, painfully, emerged from it. He had miraculously survived a 30-story leap with a few broken ribs!

"Why don't you SOB bastard go find a bridge to jump off!" Martha yelled at him. "You screwed up my car! It's worthless."

Next day Gregory read in the newspaper, "A whining New Jersey woman cursed at a young man who survived his suicidal attempt landing on her parked classic car. She had to be rescued from the fuming crowd that shouted at her, "Materialistic bitch!"

END

Hugo Hanriot

was born in Chile in 1938, and has been living in the United States since 1962. He has written in Spanish both theatre and narrative. His first novel, *Mita p'Arriba, Mita p'Abajo*, was published in 1979. His second novel, *Johnny Ortiz, Presidente de USA,* was published in 1982. In addition to the novels, Hanriot has written four plays and numerous short stories in Spanish and English.

Hugo posts every week a new fictional story based on real events at his blog –

www.stories4real.com

Made in the USA
Charleston, SC
10 April 2012